Let
Give Her More to Lose When
It's Time to Lose All . . .

Then Julie was holding the Oscar up in the air, triumphant. It was her moment. Watching from his dark room three thousand miles away, he felt electric current passing through his arms. The hate poured out of him. He imagined her silken hair coming down in two long strands, encircling her neck, strangling her.

She began to speak, and he felt the texture of her speech, soft and velvety on his skin, in his body down below . . .

When his foot went through the television screen, the set exploded in a flash of electric light.

Then the screaming began . . .

Books by Harold Lee Friedman

Crib
Don't Tell Mommy

Published by POCKET BOOKS

Most Pocket Books are available at special quantity discounts for bulk purchases for sales promotions, premiums or fund raising. Special books or book excerpts can also be created to fit specific needs.

For details write the office of the Vice President of Special Markets, Pocket Books, 1230 Avenue of the Americas, New York, New York 10020.

Don't Tell Mommy

Harold Lee Friedman

PUBLISHED BY POCKET BOOKS NEW YORK

Another *Original* publication of POCKET BOOKS

POCKET BOOKS, a division of Simon & Schuster, Inc.
1230 Avenue of the Americas, New York, N.Y. 10020

ISBN: 0-671-47257-7

First Pocket Books printing June, 1985

10 9 8 7 6 5 4 3 2 1

POCKET and colophon are registered trademarks
of Simon & Schuster, Inc.

Printed in the U.S.A.

To all mommys everywhere,
and one in particular

It's horrifying . . .
    because Julie's son is trying to kill her.
It's insane . . .
    because Julie never had a son.

Prologue
Ridgefield, Connecticut
March, 1965

THE FEELING WAS SOMETHING HE NEVER SPOKE *about. He imagined it as a dark green catfish with only one eye. Sometimes he could sense it slithering in his stomach with long tentacles that reached everywhere. It was separate from him and part of him at the same time. The feeling was his, alone, and would take hold suddenly, without warning, more powerfully than his will and more cunningly than his knowledge. And even though it hadn't surfaced recently, he knew it had been with him since the beginning, perhaps before that.*

The instant he heard the call from downstairs, he could feel the catfish moving. There was fear in his father's voice, and danger. Nevertheless, he crept to the bottom of the dim landing and cautiously turned toward the den at the end of the cavernous house.

If his father was afraid, it must be for himself, the feeling whispered.

He'd first seen the change in his father's eyes during

the winter. One day he had come home and the bright lights had gone out. No one had had to tell him something was wrong.

For a moment he felt the need to run and hide in his secret place in the cellar, but when he finally came forward and saw his father's smile, he sat down beside him and was glad.

The fire was the only light and the room smelled of smoke and rosewood. He knew being in the inner chamber was a privilege extended only to cherished friends and a son who was very much loved.

". . . and because what I have to tell you is so important," his father was murmuring, "I want you to try to understand."

The two of them moved so close they were almost touching, and he examined the outside of his father's face. With sadness he noticed new lines on his forehead and around his mouth that made him look older and more fragile. He wanted to press the lines smooth until his father looked as he once had. He suspected that if there were fewer little cracks on his face, there would be fewer in his voice, but he also knew there was nothing he could do to bring back the bright lights.

"You're more important to me than anything in the world," his father said softly. "You don't know how much that is yet, but someday you will."

The way he was saying it made him feel lonely, as if saying good–bye before a long trip.

"I'm sick. Not just a cold or the mumps or anything like that." Then he let out a sigh, waiting to see if he was being understood, and added, "The kind of sickness that isn't going to get better."

His father spoke the phrase so simply, at first the boy didn't concentrate on it. But all at once he understood, and his eyes filled.

"Never?" was the word that forced its way out.

His father shook his head back and forth slowly.

"Are you . . . going to die?"

The large white hands rose up and cupped his face between them. They were ice-cold . . . and shaking.

"Everybody dies, son . . . we have to accept it. I'm not afraid, so don't you be."

This time when he searched the eyes, he found only a half-truth, but he didn't tell his father what he saw. He was trying to imagine a day, a house, a world without him, but nothing came clear. He didn't want to listen anymore.

The now-empty words fell against his face like puffs of cool, moist wind, and he thought about his mother. She was still an idea without dimension, a picture of a pretty lady in a gold frame on the mahogany desk. She had died in childbirth, his father had told him; he knew he was to blame. But as long as he had his father, it was all right.

He was in his father's arms, pressing his head to his belly, and even in his wretchedness, he could feel the alarming thinness, the closeness of bone to skin. And then he knew that nothing he could do would change anything.

Abruptly, he pushed away from his father and stood. His hands dropped limply to his sides, and when the plea came for him to stay, he did not react. The feeling in his stomach was back. When his father's outstretched arms invited him, he shrank farther

3

away, then turned and began to walk without knowing why. He could not feel the fire any longer or smell the rosewood. He could barely see. The room had grown cold and suffocating, and his head was so full of bad thoughts he imagined himself exploding.

There was his father saying he was going to die and that he could not help. There was the thought of being completely alone. There was the picture of his mother in a gold frame on the mahogany table.

And there was the catfish in his cold belly, and the tentacles moving.

Ridgefield, Connecticut
August, 1965

DIRECTLY ACROSS THE ROOM THE BOY SAT WITH HIS *knees against his chin, his eyes fixed unwaveringly on two great French doors. Beyond the doors the lawyer sat waiting in painful silence, his arms folded across his chest, rigid, as if he believed the slightest movement might spoil the fragile peace his long-time friend had achieved.*

The older man next to him was unaware how long he'd been staring into the flames. He was remembering his son's reaction. The news changed the boy more radically than he'd thought; he'd instantly drawn into himself in unexpressed anger that seemed to worsen by the day.

Again he thought back to the beginning and the way in which his only child had come to him. The odds against his survival had been almost innumerable. Now, six years later, the miracle of it still drew him closer to thoughts of God than the science with which he filled his life.

Finally, the lawyer woefully turned to face his life-long friend and client. Even in the dim light he could see a man older than the one he knew, the slipping carriage showing the extent of his decline.

"I think it best for everyone if this happens quickly," he suggested.

A moment later the great doors opened and a nervous couple in their late twenties entered and settled onto a leather sofa.

It was a while before the woman stopped waiting for a sign of recognition and turned away from the man who just stared into the fire. One of the few things they'd heard about the famous doctor was his age—forty-four. Obviously they'd been misinformed.

"We're sorry this took so long to arrange," the lawyer said in the hushed silence. "We wanted to be sure."

The couple nodded.

"This part is quite simple." He produced several packets of paper from a briefcase. "All the required forms are now complete. There are the histories, the list of possessions, and your copy of the actual papers."

5

The trim young woman with the smooth face took them and passed them along to her husband.

"The name at the bottom is the boy's present doctor together with other acceptable ones in your own area."

The aging man put aside a twinge of pain the morphine had not been able to mask. Once more his mind went to the research he'd conducted obsessively on his son's deficiency. The work had been futile; he was unable to cure the condition except temporarily and with strong drugs. Now the wild mood swings were under control, but it was still too early to predict the extent of further problems.

". . . and with luck we can expect a normal, healthy adult," the lawyer concluded. "But with special needs."

The lawyer waited until the husband had put the lists neatly in his coat pocket. Then he paused to look at his friend as though he'd lost his bearings.

"I'm sorry. I find this difficult."

"Then I'll do it myself," the doctor answered, breaking his silence for the first time. As he spoke he stared directly at the woman, his eyes cold and deliberate.

"Within a short period of time, perhaps a few months, I want you to tell my son that his father has passed away. I want you to do this as soon as you see him adjusting to his new life."

It took a while for the couple to react.

"If you think it through," the lawyer broke in, "you may come to appreciate why it's best for the child to believe this."

For an instant the woman's eyes met the father's in an unspoken understanding. Then she looked away.

"Finally there is the matter of this letter," the legal man added wearily. He handed them a thick envelope.

"Do you want us to open it?" the husband asked. He could see it was tightly sealed, and it felt as if there were five or six pages inside.

"No. In fact, we must insist it remain in your possession, unopened, until the boy's twenty-first birthday—except under one circumstance. At that time you may decide whether to share its contents with him. The decision should be based solely on whether you believe he can benefit from what it contains."

The man and woman both wore the same confused look.

"Can't you give us some idea of what it says?" she finally asked.

"I'm sorry, no."

"Are you just trusting us not to open it?"

"Can we trust you?"

They looked at one another quickly.

"We'll respect your wish," the husband said, still gazing with astonishment at the boy's real father.

But the old doctor wasn't part of the exchange. He was looking away again, lost in the fire.

"All I can tell you is the letter outlines details of your new son's early life not important for you to know at this time. The information is entrusted to you now only in event of an emergency that cannot be remedied without it."

"What kind of emergency?"

7

DON'T TELL MOMMY

The old doctor seemed to lose patience and turned to them abruptly, with finality.

"You will know if and when the time comes."

The lawyer closed his briefcase and rose.

"If there are no further questions, once the boy and his father have had a few minutes together you may take him." He extended his hand. "Speaking for myself, I'm very glad it was you."

The boy entered the den for the last time while the couple waited beyond the closed doors where they could not hear any exchange. When he came out of the room, after only moments, he was dressed to leave. He confronted the woman squarely.

"I'm ready," he announced clearly and without the emotion she'd expected.

She stooped but did not touch him.

"I know it's hard for you to think of us as your new mother and father right now," she whispered, "so why don't we start by thinking of each other as friends? All right?"

"Yes," he answered automatically, as though he didn't care one way or the other.

"Right, buddy," the husband added as he bent down. "Just think of us as . . . as special friends."

"The boy turned his attention to the very young-looking man who loomed inches away. For just a few seconds he tried to match the eager face to the word father, but it didn't work at all.

After the three of them had driven off, the lawyer entered the den and poured two cognacs from a crystal decanter. Eventually the alcohol began to do its work.

"This must have been the hardest thing you've ever had to do, John," he said, not knowing for sure if it was a kindness or another sad reminder. "I don't know how you found the strength."

The bereft man's gaze was still lost in the dying fire. Then, with resolution, his head tilted back, he finished the last of the cognac in a single swallow.

"No," he answered, his bleak eyes fixed resolutely on his hands. "The hardest thing I ever did was bring him into this world."

DECEMBER
The Present

1
Milbrook, Connecticut

IT WAS NEARLY MIDNIGHT BY THE TIME JULIE WESton Montgomery read the Welcome to Connecticut sign in the distance and let out a cheer. She was in an airport car with her entire wardrobe in suitcases, and her outburst confirmed what the New York City limo driver had suspected all along: that the extraordinarily good-looking lady with the long, curly red hair was probably somebody famous, and definitely not running on all cylinders.

Julie was amazed to be so energized after the long flight from L.A., but a lot of things had become amazing lately. The fact that she'd just finished her second film after nearly a decade of inactivity was amazing, as was the fact that she had just been nominated for an Oscar for the first one. And most amazing of all was that after four long months of shooting, she was actually on her way home to her beloved Robert, her daughter Casey, and a perfect Connecticut Christmas.

When the limo turned off the main highway, Julie felt a knot of excitement in her stomach, and her eyes

13

strained to pick out familiar landmarks that pointed the way home. In the scant light of a crescent moon she spotted an ancient red barn that looked more ghostly than she remembered. Perhaps another winter of decay had made it so spooky, she decided.

The two-lane road wound its way up and down hills, past the condos and raised ranches built recently despite strong community objections. Most of the houses there had outside lights that would stay lit all night.

They plunged into the darkness of Milbrook's historic section where the more secure longtime locals boasted homes dating from colonial times. At this higher elevation there were still traces of the snow Robert had described in detail a few days earlier while she sweltered in the hundred-degree heat of a California desert movie location.

The solitary street lamp suddenly looming up ahead gave Julie a rush of excitement. Her driveway was just beyond it in a clearing in the trees, and at the end of the driveway was the darling 1790 saltbox home with which she and Robert had fallen in love. Six and a half acres of "man's humanity to man," as they used to joke. The house itself sat high above the driveway. Below it, they'd wired the perimeter trees with floodlights, and she was disappointed to see they weren't on. The darkness made her think of the age of the house. It was the oldest in Milbrook, and the only problem was that every so often, mostly at night, she half-expected to hear from some of the ancient, former occupants.

When they arrived, the bluestone crunched loudly

against the limo's tires, and the headlights swept the large lawn that fell away to thick woods and a brook that would now be ice. For a split second there was something out there that froze and then abruptly darted back into the blackness.

"What the hell was that?" the limo driver asked, pulling the car to a stop.

"Could be woodchuck or grizzly bear," Julie said with a straight face.

"You sure you don't want me to go up with you?" the driver said. Obviously it was the last thing on earth he wanted to do.

"Thanks, but I'll be brave," Julie said, paying him double the normal tip.

When the lights of the limo had disappeared in the distance, Julie stood in the center of a large pile of luggage, facing the clapboard house above her. She looked at it, let out a deep breath and said, "Hello, pussycat."

The wind had stopped and either the night was unusually quiet or she'd been away too long to remember the sounds of silence. Why on earth had she decided to surprise them when a grand reception would have been so gay? Standing in the cold stillness of an early Connecticut winter, she suddenly felt alone and a little strange. *Who's in there? What if something's happened? Why is the entire house dark?*

When she exhaled, a cloud of vapor issued from her lips and drifted up in front of her eyes to envelop the house in a ghostly mist. She mounted the fifteen slate steps to the stone patio she and Robert had built themselves.

She dug for the front door key they kept in the soil of a flowerbox. It was still there. With no light on the front door, she poked the metal around until the key found its slot and the mechanism clicked open. The door gave all at once with a groan that made her jump. Peering in cautiously, she could barely make out the empty den on the right, the empty dining room to the left. For some reason there were place settings on the old pine table. She drew a deep breath and quickly stepped in, closing the door before finding the light switch. Suddenly she was in absolute darkness. *Creepy!* From somewhere inside, she heard a floorboard creak, then another, and suddenly she lost her breath. Her hand feverishly worked the wall for the switch that wasn't where it should have been. When she finally found it, she jerked it up hard, and as the interior of the saltbox burst into dazzling light she began screaming hysterically.

2

THE SMALL, BONY BODY THAT JUMPED OUT FROM behind the dining room wall belonged to Artie Shore, Julie's agent and manager. His shouts of "surprise" rose well above the others'. Then she saw Mickey, her age-old buddy from New York City. A lifetime ago they'd worked together as dancers on a chorus line. Mickey Lee, alias Marsha Lansome of Salt Lake City, leaned in and with a flourish planted a kiss on Julie's cheek.

"Gotcha, JW!" she taunted.

"You crazy people," Julie roared as the full impact of a party erased the fear of a few moments before.

The happiness was running down her cheeks when her daughter, Casey, got to her with a hug.

"You little monster. Was this your idea?"

Casey was followed by Julie's sister, Margaret, up from Philly for the occasion, and finally, Robert, in a sweep-you-off-your-feet embrace that for him was too daring to perform totally sober. It felt good to be in his arms. She put her lips to Robert's ear and murmured, "I'll get you later."

The party started with an official presentation of flowers and telegrams and a giant homemade greeting card of congratulations from the crew back in Hollywood. Artie knew her too well, and had called to check up on her plans. The traitors in L.A. had told Artie about her early departure, and he'd filled in the rest to gather the partygoers a day earlier than originally planned.

Her mother was the last to come forward, proud to the point of bursting, looking as well as she had in years. Her hair was tinted blonder than usual, and when she got within a few feet of Julie she stopped, held out her arms, and made her daughter come to her, a patented move.

Later, the cork from a fourth bottle of Piper richocheted off the ceiling and disappeared magically into

17

thin air. They were all seated around a blazing fire and Julie had been commanded to sit in their midst in a pile of opened gifts, wrapping paper and ribbon. She was giddy, and couldn't stop laughing when she remembered everything she owned was still sitting in a heap in their driveway.

When Artie rose and became the evening's emcee, it took him awhile to quiet the revelers. Watching the corny but lovable little man go through his paces, Julie could still see the Borscht Belt comic he had been. Without fanfare, Artie had become one of the biggest names in agentdom.

"Okay," he said, stroking the wispy little hairs he had left on top, "it's time to turn in your homework, everybody."

Julie looked around with anticipation. "What is this, a party or third-period algebra?"

Artie rubbed his palms together. "Now let me see a show of hands. Who's gonna be first?"

Several hands went up to claim the honor.

"Good." He turned to Julie. "Everyone was given the same assignment. Come prepared with your favorite Julie story, some personal anecdote—preferably embarrassing—about their favorite actress."

"And friend," Mickey added, emphatically.

"And mother," Casey chimed in.

"And sister," from Margaret.

"And daughter," her mother decreed, triumphantly.

"Thank you, Mommy," Julie said, singsong.

"And since I'm the shy type, myself," Artie said, taking off an outrageous striped sports jacket, "I guess I'll have to lead off."

By the time they had finished booing, he'd jumped into a story about one of Julie's early auditions for a Broadway show. "She was up for a part that required acrobatic dancing, which for Julie was pushing things a bit. Let's face it, a clutz is a clutz. But ya gotta picture this," he went on. "A four-piece band, center stage at the Morosco. Backers, producers, directors, agents and this second-rate choreographer—loved to humiliate straight people—hated women—got the picture? Anyway, I'd found this terrific acrobatic coach, and Julie goes at it for seventy-two hours straight, so by the time she's called up she knows the moves but is about as nimble as Kate Smith. Well, true to form, our fussy little choreographer begins to push her. I mean, he really leans on her. Puts her through combinations, double combinations, tells her to leap higher and higher, and miraculously, she's doing it all."

"What a nice story," Julie said, cutting him off. She was already deeply crimson. "Who's got another one?"

"Until," Artie continued strongly, "she takes her final leap and suddenly loses her balance. Now get this . . . there's Julie, reeling backwards, totally out of control. The choreographer starts yelling 'cut, cut' like he's some Hollywood film director or something, but Julie's already a body in motion. So she continues backwards, past the piano player, past the trumpet, and—ready?—goes crashing, bottom first, right into the big bass drum!"

"God!" Julie said, covering her face to the uproar, "and the worst part of the story is that it's true."

"Well, everybody starts doubling up in laughter, the

19

backers, the producer, even me, everybody, of course, except the choreographer, who waits for things to quiet down, pulls himself up to his full height—about four-foot-three—and says, 'Miss Weston, in my twenty years on the stage I have never witnessed anything more ludicrous.' And without missing a beat, still plotzed in the drum, Julie answers, 'Are you trying to tell us you've *never* seen one of your own shows?' "

The room broke into wild applause.

"P.S.," Artie added, "she didn't get the job."

Mickey's hand was in the air, and she stood for her recitation.

"Careful, Lansome," Julie growled, "I got enough on you to send you to Leavenworth."

"Blackmail will get you nowhere," Mickey answered. Then she paused. "However, all things considered, I better pass." She sat back down, then stood again.

Julie's eyes did not leave her friend's face. The years had been less kind to Mickey than they might have been. She could remember vividly how she had been in the days when they'd shared a walk-up in the city. Actually, Julie had been jealous of her in the beginning. Mickey was a tall, gorgeous creature with flaxen hair that spilled halfway down her back. At five-foot-nine she stood half a head taller than Julie, and her eye-catching bosom made even her own ample curves seem trivial.

Like Julie, Mickey's desire to make a success on the stage had begun in childhood; but, ironically, her smashing appearance had been her undoing. Somehow the agents and directors could never see past the glitter to the actress underneath. Julie remembered, too, Mickey's false heroism and how afraid she'd been of the city. The adjustment from Salt Lake to Manhattan was something she'd still never really mastered. Yet, trouper that she was, she'd stayed all these years. But New York had taken its toll.

" . . . like the time she emptied a fifth of Smirnoff's into this creep's tropical fish tank," Mickey had decided to remember.

Robert took his cue. "I think our friends might like hearing about the business transaction that finally got us hitched."

For the first time Julie was genuinely perplexed.

Robert took a big gulp of champagne and was on.

"As you all know, Julie is a very deep, very sensitive spirit, despite her very large mouth. And she did some very lovely things for me after we met, especially once, after my birthday. I won't tell you which."

"Forty-six," Julie whispered loudly.

"See what I mean about the mouth?" Robert said quickly. "Anyway, Julie gave me a beautiful, romantic painting, and I was very impressed. Also, worried. In those days, she didn't have any money. Then, the next day we were at her apartment, and I accidentally happened to look at her checkbook which was still lying open on her desk. The last entry caught my eye because it was for seven hundred and some odd dollars and made out to an art gallery. Obviously, it was for the painting she bought me, but the entry completely wiped out her savings, leaving a balance of about four dollars, I think. Well, I was so touched by it, when she came out of the bedroom, I asked her to marry me."

He turned to his wife of four years. "To this day I never told you about seeing the checkbook."

Julie reached for his hand and looked at him lovingly. "I've always heard that art was a good investment."

A choir of "awwws" ended with Artie's voice: "A touching story, indeed," he said, "but let's get to the good stuff. Casey? Do you have a tidbit for us?"

Casey laughed sinisterly and moved to a cross-legged position on the couch. Julie wondered what her nineteen-year-old daughter would come up with.

"Okay, here it is. There's me and this guy in his shiny new Corvette parked about a block from here at sunset. This goes back about five years. Naturally, I was in control of the situation, but naturally, I also was not where I was supposed to be. So okay, it gets a little out of hand, and Ricky—that's his name—is giving me a hard time. All hands, y'know, but nothing serious."

"Cow chips," Julie barked, "he was trying to compromise your honor."

"And you always said people should compromise, right?" Casey said with a wink.

"Now wait a . . ."

"Anyway, so I start yelling a little, which is supposed to cool Ricky down but doesn't, and now he's backing me up against the window. Finally, I tell him if he doesn't stop I'll never see him again. Well, presto! He backs off, and I'm all kind of pleased with myself until I realize it's not me he's backing away from. See,

22

this face has suddenly risen up outside the window and it's guess who? Right: Mom . . . to the rescue. Ricky jumps straight into the air and cracks his head on the roof of the car and lets out a bloodcurdling scream. And, of course, I start laughing. 'You've been a bad boy Ricky,' Mom snarls at him, then swings open the door of the Corvette ready to kill. And that's the last time ol' Rick was heard from, which was too bad 'cause I missed the Corvette.''

"Now I ask you," Artie said, gesturing formally to Julie, "is this woman a saint or what?" He turned to Julie's mother. "Of course, Mrs. Barron, your point of view may be different."

"Yes, as a matter of fact, a good deal different." Her mother, the last of the Barrons, smiled, sipped her champagne, and began.

"So far we've heard that my daughter is clever, generous, romantic, protective and thoughtful. How many of you know that underneath all of that there's a real pain in the rear end? Take it from someone who goes way back with her. As a baby, cute. You could die from the cuteness. But the most trouble you've ever seen. Into everything. And a real daredevil, like her father, rest his soul. But the worst part was she could talk her way out of anything, especially with the men. Those eyes of hers. Weapons. Look at them. Big, blue tools of the devil."

Mrs. Barron sipped champagne again and laughed. "But like it or not, she *is* my daughter, so I might as well say I'm very, very proud of her."

The revelry continued for almost two hours before Robert finally suggested they allow Julie to rest after her long trip. When nobody moved, Julie stood and said, "Okay, beat it, you guys, the star is pooped," and everyone took the subtle hint.

Artie and Mickey waved a fond farewell from the door before beginning the drive back to New York, and the rest of the family retired to their rooms. Julie had just collapsed on the bed when the doorbell rang. It was Artie again, indefatigable, playing bellhop. He wanted to know where to put the suitcases he'd just tripped over in the driveway. And he grandly announced, with his usual twinkle, that the "Montgomerys will be hearing from my lawyer."

Moments later Julie pressed her face to the upstairs bedroom window and gaily waved Artie on his way. It was the last time she would ever see him.

JANUARY
The First Month

3
Wilton, Connecticut

IN THE SEVEN YEARS CHARLIE JOINER HAD SERVED IN the Valley Federal Savings & Loan vault department, he'd never seen anything like it. First, the woman set an endurance record by staying in the stuffy little room for almost two hours. Then she left without remembering to put away her strongbox, just left it wide open in the room. And just now, when he called after her, he might have been talking to a robot.

Charlie shrugged and made his way to the empty room, but when he saw it close-up he stopped and whistled. It was a good thing he was an honest man, otherwise he could have simply reached into that lady's strongbox and taken a few of those hundreds sticking right out in plain sight. Charlie looked around, saw that he was completely alone, and thought about it.

Mrs. Ellen Cantrell was already in the parking lot when Charlie Joiner dismissed an idea about a video cassette recorder at Reade's Department Store and placed the safe-deposit box back in the lockup. The newly discovered facts spinning around in her mind frightened her so badly she could hardly walk.

Two hours earlier she had entered the bank vault convinced that her face telegraphed the crime she was about to commit. Strangely, at that moment she remembered a dream she had had twenty years ago in high school. She was standing in front of an assembly giving a speech. Without knowing it, all the seams of her clothes had begun to unravel until she was completely naked.

Her reverie was interrupted by the guard who brought out her safe-deposit box. She smiled self-consciously, then stepped into the private cubicle, took a seat on a hard wooden chair and realized she was shivering. The door clicked shut behind her; the only sound was the whirring of a small fan she couldn't see. It was a little before one o'clock and she was scared silly.

Once she had opened the narrow steel box, it took a long time to summon the courage to reach into it. She quickly thumbed past deeds, insurance policies and other documents until her eye caught the edge of a yellow envelope at the back. She froze. Although it had been there for many years, she recognized it immediately. For a second, she felt an overpowering urge to slam the lid of the box shut again and hurry out of the room, as she had all the other times.

But this time things had finally reached the breaking point.

During the previous night's horror she had made her

decision. It was self-deception now to believe his terrible attacks would ever go away—not when they'd been increasing steadily for over a year. This time his rage had been unbridled, and for awhile she thought there was going to be blood spilled within the family. Her son had become a stranger and did things that made her physically afraid of him for the first time. At times he was like a spirit possessed by powerful forces that she didn't begin to understand. Sometimes it was visible in his face and hands, which contorted with spasms and shooting pains. Then he was like an uncontrollable, alien creature who forgot those who knew him. And there was a new malady now—the incessant foulness of his language. If she were a superstitious woman she might believe a perfectly normal child had become possessed; now, even the powerful drugs had lost much of their power to return her son to normal. And that was why this time she would not leave the room without reading whatever was inside the envelope, not if it took all day to screw up her courage to do it.

Again she thought back to the beginning when she and her husband had first met their boy. It seemed like a dream now, and she found it hard to remember he'd ever been part of another family; that they had lived through a day when they'd had to tell him his real father had died.

Picturing her son's face on that day long ago, Ellen Cantrell broke an ancient pledge and tore off one end of the envelope. Inside there were four, neatly handwritten pages, apparently copies from an original. Her

29

hands were barely useful as she separated the first page from the rest and brought the trembling paper to her eyes.

At three minutes past three, after the bank had officially closed, she put the last of the pages with the rest, folded them neatly and put them back in the envelope. She felt as if she would pass out. Moving like an automaton, she pushed back the chair, rose and steadied herself. In a few seconds she was able to tuck the letter safely in her purse and turn to the door without ever looking at the guard. A little after that, she made her way to the parking lot, shuffling like a blind person and desperately trying to fight back the tears welling in her eyes.

Nothing in Ellie Cantrell's life would ever be the same.

4

Milbrook, Connecticut

IT HAD BEEN A SEASON, A FILM, AND TEN THOUSAND miles since she'd last seen candlelight in Robert's eyes.

The restaurant he picked was typical of the area, spartanly furnished, yet cozy and romantic in its simplicity. She wanted someplace they'd never been because it was a night for new beginnings, to be shared with Robert slowly, like sipping fine wine. The day had been filled to brimming. Her autobiography, tentatively titled *The Has-Been*, was off to a flying start, and the exciting mental buzz she woke with each morning was getting louder. Lately she'd come to think of her imagination as an alarm clock that never needed winding. The book was another project, one of the many she kept going and seemed to need all the time. It had been that way ever since she could remember, and she no longer cared to examine the reason. Activity was what made her tick, made her Julie Weston.

Except that today her entire active schedule had gone out the window by ten-thirty.

Julie looked across the table at Robert and debated which piece of news to tell him first. One was going to make him angry, the other was impossible to predict. Typically, despite her anxiousness, she'd been talking non-stop about other things since the moment they'd sat down. Sometimes she felt like ten people all rolled into one, all going in different directions.

Without fanfare, she suddenly held out two tightly-clenched fists to him.

"There's good news and bad news. Take your pick."

Robert was used to her flair for the dramatic, and tapped her left fist with only moderate interest.

She winced. "Now don't get crazy, but someone gave me a bit of a hard time at the house today."

Robert's face instantly darkened. Her safety at home was one of their most frequent topics. In his mind she was stuck out in the middle of nowhere,

31

vulnerable and alone. The thought never left him while he was at his advertising agency, and he occasionally went into diatribes about the careless things she did. In other words, he loved her a lot.

His thick, dark eyebrows narrowed, but he waited for more information.

"I was just out of the shower when the doorbell rang. I figured it was Lillian Cross from down the road so I threw a robe on and went to the front door."

"Was it locked?" Robert had to know right away.

"I only opened it a crack at first because it was so cold this morning, but by the time I got there there was no one around. I didn't know how long they'd been waiting, so I figured they gave up and left."

Robert's concerned expression did not soften. He put down his fork, looked at her, and waited.

"When I heard the knocking at the back door I wasn't really suspicious, but there was no one there again, so I got a little irritated. It still could have been innocent, but I had the feeling that someone was playing a trick. Anyway, I pushed the door open and leaned out for a better look. And that's when it happened."

"What happened? For crying out loud, Julie . . . "

"I know this is going to sound weird, but all of a sudden there were these . . . ugly, big hairy spiders. In my hair, on my face, all over me." She shuddered at the memory of it and reached for his hand. "But it turned out to be some kind of practical joke. The spiders were those phony kind, all soft plastic, but very realistic. God, I've always hated spiders. Someone had rigged a gadget over the door that dropped

32

them on me when I opened it. I should have known there aren't any spiders in winter, but anyway it obviously took some planning."

"You think it was that local kid? The retarded one?"

"The Gillick boy? Joseph? He's not retarded, just slow."

"Whatever." Robert shook his head. His eyes were full of agitation—and anger.

"You want to hear the rest? I haven't got to the mental anguish part."

"Goddammit, Julie," he snapped. "The day I can get one serious conversation out of you is the . . . "

"Sorry. Okay, so after I realized it was a joke I threw on a coat, wrapped my hair in a towel and went outside to look. God, it was cold. Naturally, I couldn't find anybody, but I did hear someone running away. Also, there was a sound like a box of candy shaking. By the time I got back to the house I was steaming." Julie stopped abruptly, hesitant to go on. "And that's when I found this."

She reached into a sweater pocket, withdrew a crumpled piece of paper and held it out. Robert unfolded it quickly and read. It was written in a child's scrawl.

ALONG CAME A SPIDER
AND SAT DOWN BESIDE HER
AND SCARED THE PISS OUT OF MOMMY

It was written on notebook paper, from a school composition book. It was unsigned.

"What do you think it means?" Julie asked. "I mean the *mommy* part."

Robert let out a deep breath and tried to let the anger flow out of him. "You got some little ones running around I don't know about?"

Julie plucked out a sugar packet and threw it at him. Yet the *mommy* thing actually did stir an old and painful memory. It forced her to think about her first marriage almost fifteen years before when she had almost become a mommy for the second time. After she'd had Casey, things had gone rapidly downhill with TJ; but that hadn't stopped her from getting pregnant again. In those days it was more serious, because abortion was still a dirty word. The search for a doctor whom she could trust had been hard and sometimes humiliating, but she had finally located one through friends in show business and he had performed the relatively simple operation in his office. The trouble was, somehow, TJ had found out. The episode had brought on the fateful argument that eventually led to their breakup.

Robert interrupted her unpleasant reverie. "I think we'll let the police try to figure this out." He rubbed at his eyes wearily. "It's that damn Gillick kid, I know it."

"And if it isn't, we'll destroy the whole neighborhood with a false accusation. Uh, uh. Maybe we'd just better let it go, unless there's a repeat performance. Maybe if I don't react, whoever did it won't get enough jollies to do it again."

"Jesus, Julie," Robert said sternly, "why did you go and tell me if you don't want to do anything about it?"

His hand went into the air, signaling the waiter for the check. The wonderful dinner she'd planned was nearing an end.

"Only because you picked the wrong hand, you fool."

In the midst of his turmoil her face had taken on an elfish grin; she held out the other hand.

When he didn't want to play the game she opened it, anyway. "If you had chosen this one I'd have been compelled to tell you we're going to have a baby."

Slowly Robert lowered his hand. His mouth remained open.

FEBRUARY
The Second Month

5

A PURE, DAZZLING BLANKET OF WHITE LEFT THEIR small community buried under a foot and a half of soft snow. It was perfect timing because Casey was in from Wellesley for a rare weekend appearance. In fact, when Julie went downstairs very early, she was surprised to see Casey already in front of the window, looking out. It was no small accomplishment, considering the two of them had stayed up past two waiting for the first flakes. A storm on the way was one of the excitements they still shared, like two schoolgirls awaiting prom night; love for the natural world was something Julie had always liked in her daughter.

Unfortunately, Julie hadn't found a way the night before to tell Casey the baby news; the prospect made her nervous, although she wasn't exactly sure why.

As soon as Julie suggested they go outside, Casey was moving. It took about two seconds for them to throw on boots, coats and mufflers, and once they were knee deep in the fluffy powder, they shared a moment of silent wonder. It was just past eight on a Saturday morning and the roads were plowed, but empty. Everywhere they looked the branches and bushes had a thick white coat and it was much too cold for melting. The air was still and sweet with the scent of a hardwood fire. In the wake of the storm Julie traced a special sensation and remembered it was the way she had felt in church when she was a little girl. Later, when they were warm from a half-mile walk, Casey suddenly stopped short and turned to her mother.

"Would you like to tell me now, or do you want me to guess?"

Julie, taken off guard, laughed awkwardly.

"I may have been away to school for a while but I haven't forgotten what it means when you go quiet. It always used to precede some big announcement. So, am I right?"

A caught-in-the-act smile spread across Julie's face. Casey was always good at reading her moods; luckily, the converse was true as well.

"Well, Ms. Phi Beta Brilliant, you're right. But if you're so damned brilliant you'll have to guess."

Casey smiled. "Wouldn't be far off if we talked movies, I'll bet. You got a new one? Or are you up for another Oscar, maybe?"

"Go to the rear of the class."

"Nothing to do with the movies?"

Julie shook her head.

Casey frowned and turned to watch the first cautious car of the morning slowly pass. An unknown driver waved as he plowed by. Friendly little town.

"I don't get the feeling it's bad news, that's for sure."

Instinctively Julie held out a mittened hand and drew Casey toward her. "What would you say if I told you that you're going to have a new brother or sister?"

Julie's smiling eyes did not leave Casey's as her face registered the shock.

"You're going to have a . . . a baby?" she asked incredulously.

"Happens to the best of us. What do you think?"

"Is this for real? A baby? You?"

"I just found out for sure a few days ago. I wanted to be certain before I got everybody excited for nothing. And last night I just felt a little shy about telling you."

"Do you want one? Now that everything is going so well?"

"Of course I do. I think we're a family again and a pretty terrific one, so why not add another member? Besides, I want a baby with Robert. He means a lot to me . . . to us, doesn't he?"

"Well, sure," Casey said, surprise still clear in her voice.

They walked several more paces before Julie spoke, feeling that she was making an apology.

"I hoped it would be happy news for you, but I knew it might be quite a shock, as well." Julie paused for a moment. "Do you think I'm silly to be having a baby at my age?"

"If the doctors say its all right I don't think forty is any big deal."

"Good, I appreciate that. I'm not sure, however,

that Robert feels the same way. He seems to think forty is a *very* big deal." Julie laughed and Casey joined her.

They turned back toward the house, walking mittened hand in mittened hand. When the saltbox came into view, framed in snow, Robert was out on the patio. They'd been gone a long time and he was hunched over, looking for them. When he spotted Julie's red parka he waved exuberantly.

Julie felt herself beam in response. And then, suddenly, she was serious. "You know, Casey, it hasn't been that easy for Robert. You made it tough on him when he tried to be a father to you. But he loves you, you know."

"I know he does. And I think we're getting there."

"I know. And that makes me very happy."

"By the way, what exactly does Robert think about the baby?" Casey asked.

They stopped one last time in the driveway. Robert waved again, beckoning them, then scurried inside.

"He cried," Julie said simply. "When I told him, he cried."

Casey smiled at her mother and squeezed her hand.

"I told him last night at dinner," Julie continued. "I wouldn't have believed it but the great stone face cracked."

Casey smiled again, then suddenly turned and hugged her mother. "A little brother or sister," she murmured. "Wow, that's great. Really great."

Julie hugged her daughter back, then said, softly, "Let's get inside before Robert has a fit. I think we're gonna have your basic worrywart, overly protective father-to-be on our hands."

Casey grinned at that, and hand-in-hand they walked the rest of the way up the driveway back to the house.

6

JULIE GLARED AT THE BROKEN COFFEE MUG AND told herself everyone had days like the one she was having; it had nothing to do with being pregnant. That morning she had awakened at a slight distance from the world, a fine gauze between her eyes and reality.

She was more skittish than usual, like a cat that wakes up spooked for no apparent reason. Even small noises seemed to jolt her senses; she was dropping things right and left. To make matters worse she'd been thumbing through the family album and some of her favorite pictures were missing, probably taken surreptitiously by Mom, who'd always harbored a larcenous interest in them. It was a good day to stay in bed, but that wouldn't be fair to Mickey.

This was their third try, since the party, at getting together in New York. It was Mickey's only matinee day of the week, and this time she'd made no secret about how important it was to her. She'd told Julie to come backstage after the show and that meant she was anxious to show off her successful friend to fellow performers. It made Julie remember the pledge made years before that whoever made it first would help the other.

But there was nothing on which she could directly pin her unusual tension. Now, near the beginning of the third month, she was still not suffering from the afflictions often visited upon women at that stage of pregnancy. The few bouts of morning sickness, which actually came at mid-afternoon, were easily countered with small amounts of dry food, as the doctor had advised on her first visit, until the hormonally-caused stomach problem passed. Lethargy, another common complaint, wasn't a problem, either. In fact, she had an excess of energy and wondered whether that meant something was wrong. Her breasts had become tender and swollen, however, to a greater degree than she remembered from her first pregnancy. She already resented the imprisonment of the larger, reinforced bras.

But there was one plus that came out of being pregnant, besides the baby itself: a decrease in the number of her migraines. So far she hadn't suffered any, and that was cause for celebration. In any case, by noon she'd already drunk half her daily quart of milk and taken her iron pills, and there was nothing in Dr. Bain's printed list that prevented her from appearing in the audience of the Greer Theater on Forty-sixth Street in New York City at 2:30 P.M.—even if the spooky feeling came along for the ride.

A front-row ticket was waiting for her at the box office, as promised. It had been a long time since she had been merely a member of an audience without being there to scout a part. Mickey's show, *Kitty*, was a new-wave musical, based loosely on the life and times of Kit Carson, the frontier cowboy. The concept was as radical as the treatment. It was staged as a dance-farce, whatever that was, and the hook of the show was that Carson had in actuality been a male impersonator, a macho female type who dressed in cowboy drag. The critics had chosen to pan the production, while actually liking the premise.

Watching Mickey perform in the line of radicalized frontier women, Julie felt pride in her friend's courage and admiration for her dancing ability. There was even a fleeting pang of jealousy for not being up there with her. But in the end, the emotion that came on strongest was sympathy. After so many years of trying, Mickey was still a chorus line hoofer, sweating a lot and getting nowhere. It made Julie sad to think about what might have been, and when the curtain came down to only polite applause, she stood and cheered Mickey's name loudly, as those around her stared.

She first started to feel the dizziness after the drink they had between shows at the Lido Bar. Probably it was the wine spritzer and nothing more, except that it brought on a return of the feeling she had had earlier and made her very woozy. She hadn't mentioned it, when Mickey suddenly looked at her watch and jumped up, late for the next performance. A few moments later, outside in the early darkness of a city winter, she watched her friend turn for the back door

45

of the theater and disappear. Then, walking down the block of illuminated marquees, Julie suddenly felt deeply ill.

It was like the weakness that preceded a major flu, only more in the core of her body. Before long, as she slowed her pace, the automotive exhaust in the air became oppressive and the theater lights swam in her vision. She could feel the beads of sweat forming on her forehead, even in the below-freezing temperature, and the insides of her fur-lined gloves were sopping when she rested near the entrance of the last theater, only steps from the tumult of Times Square. That area was obviously no place to be alone on any night, let alone in her current state.

The first possible explanation for the condition was food poisoning, but aside from the single drink and a couple of hors d'oeurves she'd had with Mickey, there was nothing that could have done it. A second thought suddenly filled her with terror: *I'm losing the baby.* Without anything else to account for her sudden illness, the idea was all too real, initiating a new sweep of nausea. She could feel her legs buckling and it was getting dark rapidly. In the midst of thousands of strangers she suddenly needed someone to help her, someone to carry her to a doctor who'd make the feeling of aching loss in her belly go away.

For a moment she drifted back in memory. She was in the rented ground-floor apartment in Sheepshead Bay with TJ. The labor had stopped after an intense cramp; she was wishing it would never return, that she wouldn't have to bring a baby into their desperate

world. Then a curtain in her mind fell and rose and she
was in Connecticut with the practical joker at the door.
His face was covered with spiders crawling in and out
of eyes and mouth. Then she was back in the present
on the street and saw people staring at her. She tried to
speak, but couldn't. No one knew what to do for her;
no one came forward to offer help. Then one of three
Spanish youths passed by and came forward, close,
the biggest one, and whispered something filthy in her
ear. All of a sudden she was screaming, though she
heard the sound as if through a long, narrow tunnel.

That was when her legs gave way completely and
she slumped to the pavement. The last thing she felt
was the blood oozing between her legs and she knew it
was the end of the life in her womb—the end of her
baby.

Julie had regained consciousness by the time the
police arrived and helped her into a squad car, and in
the next few minutes her strength surged back. Miraculously, before long, she felt almost completely normal again. The dizziness, the hot flashes, the nausea,
everything had vanished, even the disconnected sensations. The only remaining fear was that she'd returned to life at the expense of her baby.

As the police gently questioned her, she could imagine Robert's reaction to her New York trip. She could
see the pain he'd be forced to relive with her, and she
could hear his anger at her having taken unnecessary
chances. She'd need all her wits to calm him. For the
time being, she had to convince the two officers she

was recovered enough for them to let her off at her parking garage. As far as she could tell, the bleeding had stopped, but she still had to get to a doctor she trusted and not to an emergency ward as suggested by the two young cops.

The officers reluctantly dropped her off at the parking garage, and the single call she made before her car came down was to Bain's office in Danbury. By luck, she caught him before he was about to leave, and after hearing about her sudden sickness, he agreed to wait the hour or so it would take for her to drive up. He also commanded her not to drive by herself, an order to which she agreed, and then promptly ignored.

An hour and a half later Julie appeared in his waiting room, drained, scared and feeling as if she wanted to crawl into a hole and die.

"I've lost the baby," she said as a simple statement of fact. "I don't know how or why, but I lost it."

Bain ignored her, and asked a number of quick questions. There was no further exchange until he poked and probed, and examined a blood sample. Only after an eternity had passed did he venture an opinion.

"I beg to differ with you, Julie."

She felt tears forming in her eyes.

"Tell me," he continued, "did you experience any focused pain? Abdominal cramps, anything like that?"

Julie stared at the sixty-year-old obstetrician who had suddenly begun to take on godlike proportions; she was grateful for her luck in having him. She found herself wanting to hug him.

"Anything like that?" Bain repeated.

"No," she stammered. "Just dizzy with hot flashes. And a feeling that something had gone wrong inside."

Bain straightened up with a smile.

"As far as I'm concerned, you have nothing to worry about. There's nothing in what you went through that indicates a miscarriage. The dizzy spell and hot flashes are common, as you know. Perhaps the wine and the excitement combined to cause a bad reaction. You probably thought you could take more than you could. It's something you're going to have to watch a bit more carefully from now on."

"What about the bleeding?"

"It happens," Bain said, "in the first few months, and is little cause for alarm unless the flow is heavy and prolonged. From what I can see I'd say it was more like heavy spotting. Again, perhaps it was because of your emotional state at the time. Excesses in emotion are to be expected, now."

"Especially for someone given to them in the first place. Is that what you're thinking?"

Bain smiled. "What—Julie Weston given to displays of emotion? Who would suggest such a thing?"

"So there's nothing to really be worried about?"

Bain nodded and reached for her file. "As far as your medical history goes, there's no reason whatever for concern. Not that it's perfect, but nobody's ever is. There's no history of diabetes or heart or kidney disorders, none of the so-called serious problems. Physically, you're in good shape to bear a baby; far better than most women your age. Naturally the fact that you've already given birth is in your favor." He folded his arms and seemed genuinely pleased. "You don't smoke or drink heavily, you don't take any long-term medications, and you're not under any long-term stress. Practically," he smiled again, "a perfect patient."

Again Julie had the urge to hug the kindly doctor.

"As a matter of fact, there are only one or two things I'm at all concerned about, one of them being your weight."

Julie grimaced, automatically. She'd had trouble sticking to Bain's diet and had gained eight pounds after less than two months.

"I know," she said sheepishly. "I'll be better from now on. I didn't think I could put it on as fast as I did, maybe because as a kid I used to have to drink malteds and eat pasta to gain an ounce."

"You're not the kid you used to be. Of course," Bain patted his round stomach, "none of us are. You know, metabolism, and all that stuff doctors love to talk about. Remember, our target is between twenty and twenty-five pounds for the full term, and you've already gained almost half of the lower amount in just two months."

She nodded. His order wasn't going to be all that hard to fill. She knew her will power was mighty, once there was a good reason to exercise it, and she'd never had a better reason.

Julie pushed herself off the table feeling strong—and very, very relieved.

"And where do you think you're going?" Bain asked with sudden sternness. His hand was on her elbow pushing her back.

"What's the matter?"

"I said two things were on my mind and your weight was only the first. There's something else I want to check."

"Why do I feel like an automobile all of a sudden?" Julie said, smiling. She laughed out loud, but watching her doctor, she spotted the subtlest of changes, as though there was a flash of real concern behind the banter. "Is something going on I need to worry about?"

"Don't worry about anything until I tell you to."

Julie braced; nothing was as worrisome as a doctor saying there was nothing to worry about.

"You're not trying to protect me all of a sudden, are you," Julie asked, "because of my emotional tendencies?"

"Nonsense," Bain answered. "Now just roll up your sleeve. I've got some work to do."

A few minutes later, after a test he had performed twice before, Bain's buoyant mood had darkened noticeably.

I was right, Julie thought. I was right all along: something *is* wrong.

7
New York City

NOT MANY PEOPLE UNDERSTOOD THAT NEARLY PER-
fect recall was a curse disguised as a blessing. It
brought back moments of terror and pain with total
clarity. Now, safe behind the locked door of his upstairs bedroom, he remembered vividly the events
leading up to the hellish discovery of the week before,
as though still hearing the echo of a scream just
uttered.

There were many things he'd hated about the trip
into New York City that Thursday afternoon, and the
cold windswept rain was one of the minor ones. He
also abhorred returning to the most painful reminder
of his search for help, the hemotologist who'd promised so much in the beginning and failed in the end like
the others. But, again, he found himself making his
way to the Fifth Avenue blood specialist he hadn't
seen for almost a year. More than anything, it was the
need in himself that he despised, the weakness of false

hope that kept him going to doctors when he knew there was nothing to be learned except what color his new pills would be.

As usual, he'd come alone to the exclusive address. He was getting used to being alone and even took solace from the fact that fewer people were now close to him. There were really two parts to him: the outward one, starting to show the deterioration beneath, and an ugly inner part, which was better kept to himself. There was no longer any question that he was different. The only issue left was how different.

A plaque on the familiar luxury apartment house bore the name Claire Astinow, M.D. He lingered outside in the cold rain, conjuring a mental picture of the physician. She was a cool lady in her early forties who stood chin high to him and had a pretty, alabaster face and long shapely legs under her white gown. He'd never seen her in anything but the gown, but many times he'd imagined what lay underneath. Someday he knew he would take the antiseptic white garment in both hands and rip it to the waist; then the real examination would begin.

He reached for the brass plaque on the building and traced the raised letters on it. Among her fellow specialists, he had been reassured, Claire Astinow was a famous name. There probably wasn't a hemotologist in the country who didn't look forward to one of the Astinow papers in the *Journal of Medicine* every year. But with all her success, all the times she'd taken blood, x-rayed, scanned and examined all parts of his body, the humiliation was without the slightest benefit.

The hard truth was that he had worsened every visit, although, of course, *everyone* had said it was just the opposite. The spasms came more often now, and the crazy feelings never left him for long, despite all her efforts to control them. So when he entered the lavish offices and ended up on the examination table again, he waited for her with absolutely no expectations.

As usual, the appointment had been his mother's idea, and he'd thought it was an unkind thing to ask of him after all he'd been through. Before she'd brought it up again he had been under the impression that she'd finally given up on Astinow, too, but her recent surprise request had come with so much conviction, he'd finally acquiesced. The conversation had left him feeling there was something his mother wasn't saying, and he'd noticed she'd had trouble looking him in the eye while they spoke. Perhaps it was only her embarrassment from raising his hopes again, but he couldn't deny that after fifteen years, he still clung to the hope himself, even though he knew his parents had already spent a fortune; even though he still felt as if he came from Mars.

He was considering this last thought when the slim lady doctor entered the room and asked him to strip to the waist. Afterward, as usual, Astinow consulted his medical records on a clipboard without looking at him, and there was no exchange until she looked up and smiled artificially.

"Well, you look healthy. How have you been feeling since the last time?"

His eyes drilled her with antagonism. He was sick of the phony preliminaries and wanted her to know it.

"The medication needs to be increased," he said evenly. "The attacks are getting worse."

"Worse in what way?" she asked, and he could tell she didn't believe him or didn't want to.

He shrugged. *I've told you a hundred times. It's worse. Worse means worse. Bad. Horrible.*

She put down her pad and walked closer to the table on which he sat.

"Come on now, if you don't help me we're not going to get very far."

Very far. What a joke. "What do you want to know?"

"How many episodes have you had in the last six months? How long do they last? Do they feel any different from before?"

His attention drifted from the conversation to the swell of the white gown where her breasts fought the fabric. He thought of an *episode* she would never forget.

"A few every month, but more lately. They're lasting longer, too. One of them took two hours before it was over."

"And the new medication? Is it helping?"

I already said they're worse, you stupid bitch.

"Not as much as it used to," he responded coldly. "And it takes longer to work."

Why am I here? What's the use? Nothing will change.

"Okay, I want to tell you what we're going to do this time." Astinow took off her glasses and began tapping the pad in front of her. Whenever she took that pose, she added extra coldness to her manner.

55

"It's something new and I don't know how much it's going to tell us, but it's worth a try."

He checked an involuntary reaction that began to take him toward hopefulness. *Nothing will ever change.*

Dr. Astinow moved closer to him until he could smell a faint perfume that reminded him of honeysuckle; she looked at him in a way that made him sense still another deception was coming.

"It's going to take some courage on your part. Are you up to it?" She stared imperiously at him, her eyes cold as ice.

Don't you know it takes courage just to get up in the morning?

"Up to what?" he said wearily.

"I want to monitor your blood counts over a period of time, say four hours, while we do something to induce a change. If the change is great enough, we may be able to read something we haven't seen before."

A shiver shot up his spine. *You can't mean what I think you mean.*

"Would you agree to an artificially induced attack right now? Right here in the office?"

His hands gripped the edge of the table tightly as the hot panic rose up from his bowels. *Fuck off!* a voice inside him screamed out.

"Take it easy," she said, seeing his reaction. "This is a voluntary test I'm suggesting. If after we talk about it you don't want to, I won't make you."

No shit, bitch. I'd kill you first.

With great effort he held himself in check. "What's the point? What are you looking for?"

She braced noticeably at this most obvious of questions.

"I'll be honest with you, maybe nothing. But I've done some research on your history and I have a new idea, actually a very specific idea of what to look for. It's too complicated to get into," she said, starting to reach for his shoulder but stopping short of actual contact. "Besides, you'd need a master's in chemistry to understand."

He studied her eyes, daring her to avert his, and, of course, she broke first.

You're not telling me the truth. You've always failed, but at least you always told me the fucking truth before.

"What made you think of it now . . . after all this time?"

"Let's just say I got lucky."

"Luck," he snorted, "that's great."

The look on her face was suddenly sympathetic. "I think we know enough now about what brings on an episode to simulate it with the right chemicals. We can induce a diabetic attack with insulin, for example. I know it sounds a little scary, but if we can get you into one of your seizures and watch what happens to your blood, we may be able to isolate a specific treatment. An antidote, if we're fortunate."

A little scary? Try fucking nightmarish!

"One thing to remember is that you're here, and if we can get you into it, we can get you out."

When I'm in it, seconds are hours. It's like being trapped on a runaway roller coaster. The Cyclone at the amusement park.

"Suppose it's one of the long ones?" he pleaded, hating the whine he heard in his own voice.

She smiled her phony, supposedly reassuring smile.

"Don't worry. I've set aside as much time as we need. Now what do you say we do some research?" Again the smile flashed.

Fuck yourself, bitch.

"I . . . I have to think about it."

"All right," she said as though she knew she was going to win. "Why don't you think it over for a few minutes while I quickly check on another patient. What we might have to gain and whether it's worth a few minutes of discomfort is your decision. While you're thinking, I'll ask my nurse to take another blood sample for your records. Okay?" The awful smile flashed again and she started to reach for him, stopped, and turned to leave. His eyes fell on the perfect roundness of her buttocks. For an instant the split near the bottom of her gown opened and he spotted a section of gauzy stocking and the promise of milky flesh underneath.

Maybe if you let me stick it in you I'll do it. Maybe that would be worth a little discomfort.

A black nurse entered the moment Astinow left and put a long needle in the vein of his right arm. He watched his own blood fill a flat, calibrated syringe and wondered if the blood, itself, was the source of the evil that haunted him. *How much longer can you stand this?* After the nurse left he felt diminished from the loss of blood. But compared to the roller coaster, it was nothing. Everything was nothing, compared to the Cyclone.

In the silence of the room he again tried to picture what lay underneath Astinow's white gown, but suddenly he saw his mother's face and remembered how she'd pressed him to go back to the doctor. There had been a pitying quality in her voice during that conversation.

She knew something. Found out something. That's why I'm here. The idea struck with such simple logic and power that it was irresistible. If there was something hidden, it would be written down somewhere, and it might be here in the office. His eyes swept the room for the clipboard, but couldn't find it. Listening for anyone approaching, he quietly opened the two drawers beneath a built-in countertop, then the adjacent cabinets, but there was nothing there. As he edged back toward the table, he concluded that any important data would be in her office, and he instantly reversed direction and put his ear to the adjoining door leading to her office. There was no sound; he cracked the door open and found no one. Alone, he breathed in her scent, then scanned the plushly appointed office without moving. It was filled with artifacts he remembered in detail from other visits: delicate vases so ornately decorated, they had to be centuries old; the shiny antique desk and glittering Tiffany lamp; the lovely oil paintings his parents' hard-earned money had helped to buy.

He went directly to a set of wooden file cabinets, surprised that he did not feel the least bit nervous. He began going through the files, his fingertips brushing the tops until he found his own.

A noise outside the office stopped him abruptly, but

he did not move and a moment later the sound was gone.

The thick file spanned eight years of his medical history. In all that time Astinow had never changed the records, so that many were now yellowed with age. He rushed through the paper, scanning quickly, precisely, until he came to a page with the heading "Prognosis." After the usual medical terminology, at the bottom of the page, in pencil, was the phrase: "Reversal doubtful."

As the terse, cold condemnation registered, he felt the blood rush to his head and begin to pound.

Crazy is what she's saying. Crazy! Then why put me through the tests; why put me through an "episode"? A guinea pig. For a new medical journal paper. Bitch, you goddam bitch!

His rage built as he stared down at the simple words, "Reversal doubtful." He picked up the file with trembling hands and slipped it back in its proper place. As he did, he spotted a yellow envelope tucked deep in the folder and plucked it out. He saw his mother's name on it and felt a spear enter his side. He slowly opened the envelope and removed four yellowed pages that looked as though they'd been folded and refolded many times.

When he'd finished reading the four pages, his entire body was vibrating. His eyes flashed to his right hand and saw the old gold watch he never took off. The "last" gift. It bore an inscription that until that moment had been his only connection with the past. He forced himself to his feet, electricity racing through his body and, suddenly, something inside him snapped.

*   *   *

There was a terrible scream. And then the crashing sounds. Glass breaking. By the time Claire Astinow had burst into her office, it was empty. She heard steps pounding away down a long hallway, a shout, a slapping sound and then another crash. Finally she heard the waiting room door smashing open against the wall with a shuddering crack.

She looked down with tears in her eyes at the two thirteenth century vases she'd bought at Sotheby's— or what was left of them.

8

Milbrook, Connecticut

JULIE ANGLED HER BODY SO THAT HER BREAST JUST barely touched Robert's naked bicep. He inhaled her perfume and let out a sigh.

"It's not going to work," he reported, his brown eyes quickly darting to meet hers, "not until I'm convinced we're doing the right thing. I think you've been evasive about what Bain told you last time. Maybe you're doing it to protect me, but I don't like it. I don't want to be protected."

Julie saw the set of his jaw, the thick, furrowed eyebrows, and knew she had lost. Quickly she turned her own thoughts to the most recent visit with Dr. Bain. He'd alarmed her with a definite warning, a warning that had been constantly on her mind ever since.

"I don't see what you're so upset about," she tried. "Lots of women over forty have babies. It's a little harder, but no big deal."

Robert propped himself up on his elbow and faced her. "You know how I feel. If there's the slightest chance you're going to be put in danger . . ."

"Robert, do me a favor, will you?" she interrupted. "Don't start inventing problems that don't exist. I know how much you care, but you'll only get yourself worried for nothing. And that'll make me more worried than I need to be."

Robert didn't answer; concern was etched on his face like a mask.

"Hey, c'mon," she said, threatening his exposed ribcage with a long, pointed finger.

He tried to smile but it was easy to see that Dr. Bain's warning had scared him, not to mention the incident in New York.

Robert's intense concern for her well-being had been present from the beginning of their history together, and by the end of their first year his protectiveness had become one of the hallmarks of their relationship. Now, like his loyalty to her, it had only intensified with marriage. Julie remembered how astonishing it had been in the early days to see him in action on her behalf, the way he'd taken her side in arguments with friends or relatives, only to find out later he disagreed with the position he'd helped her defend.

She'd always believed Robert was a good deal brighter than she was. His mind worked like a computer, able to outdistance hers and arrive at the correct conclusions, like a chess player who operated five moves ahead of his opponent. Robert was basically a planner, though, and he needed lieutenants to carry out his plans. Julie used to muse that they would make a good pair in the Pentagon: he mapping the strategy, she dealing with tactics.

Yet in certain situations Robert was a babe in the woods. For such a successful man, he was still socially awkward, sweet, but uptight with strangers and, like a child, quite capable of shyness. Thus, although able to write the most wonderful speech and deliver it beautifully, once he had left the podium, he became bashful and reserved. Most of the time his liability was misconstrued as quiet thoughtfulness, but Julie knew the truth. Robert was afraid of people he didn't know personally. And once she understood this central fact about him it was easier to understand his fear for her. Someone like the practical joker with the spiders wasn't just an obnoxious prankster to him; it confirmed his worst suspicions about people.

Yet the result of his over-caring wasn't very hard to take. For the most part Robert controlled his protectiveness, and a day never passed without Julie knowing that she could always depend on his support. In the end, there weren't many other qualities in a person that mattered much more. Not only did she love Robert, but she had realized one day long ago that she also felt utterly safe with him.

"The point really comes down to this," she said finally, deliberately abstracting their discussion, "everything of value comes with risk, and the greater the value, often the greater the risk." Then, realizing she'd chosen exactly the wrong way to say it, she added quickly, "But mine isn't that much greater than even much younger mothers'."

Robert closed his eyes and sighed. "That's the part I have trouble with, the isn't-that-much-greater part. What is that supposed to mean? How much greater?"

Julie drew back and looked directly at Robert. "I'll make a deal with you. If I can persuade you that in six months I'm going to be a proud and healthy mommy, will you put it out of your mind and shut up and ravage me?"

At the end of her offer she was face to face with him, comically batting long, dark eyelashes.

"Maybe," he allowed, not weakening entirely under the onslaught, "but I want it all, okay? No holding back, Julie. We're a partnership here, and that means we make important decisions together."

"Deal!" she said, sitting up and adjusting a pillow behind her back. "Now let me start with a question: Who's the biggest chicken you ever met in the whole wide world?"

He was smiling, finally.

"You," he granted, "no contest."

"Correct. So, number one, from what I've learned, am I acting afraid? Do I seem worried? No! So far I've been told to expect a normal pregnancy and probably less trouble with the actual delivery than with Casey, which wasn't bad at all." That part was a small white lie. Casey *had* come easily, but only after a twenty-hour labor. "I'm sure even that great advertising mind of yours has heard it's easier the second time around."

"Even if the first baby was almost twenty years ago?"

"Absolutely, according to Dr. Bain." Then she grinned. "And thanks for reminding me about the time."

She watched him struggle and made an easy guess.

"My age *is* really what's bothering you, isn't it?"

"Yes it is. I know you're still a young woman in so many ways but not . . ."

"Not in *that* way," Julie completed. "Well, you're right, it's a fact that I'm forty. But medical opinion has changed since the old days, and by old days I mean just a decade or so ago. It used to be that once a woman hit forty, doctors got real nervous, but not now."

"Is that what Bain is saying?"

"Absolutely. He says there's a bit of extra risk, of course, but not that much. For one thing the health of women in general has improved. Today's forty-year-old is in much, much better shape than yesterday's." Julie gave him a telling look. "And this forty-year-old is even better. Right?"

"Bain said that?"

"He sure did. And for another thing, medicine has improved. There are tests now that didn't exist in my mother's day. Early warnings have been developed for almost anything that might go wrong with the mother or baby, like the amniocentesis that's coming up soon. Plus, there are new drugs to correct conditions that used to complicate late pregnancies."

"Jesus," he said resignedly. "Julie, you're impossible."

She grinned. "Did you know there was a woman in England who gave birth in her eighties, and one in South America who had her fifteenth baby in her fifties? Truth."

"Okay, okay, just as long as you're not saying there's no limit, because that's gotta be crazy."

"Of course not. But forty is safe. And there are plenty of safeguards. Besides, Dr. Bain loves my cervix."

Robert softened completely. "Talking dirty will get you nowhere," he muttered under his breath.

"And if it makes you feel any better about how safe it is, you'd be surprised to hear the list of things I'm allowed to do, right up until the delivery."

"Oh, yeah?"

"Yeah." Her right hand started moving up her body and came to the strap of her nightgown.

"I can still swim in the pool all I want . . ."

"In February?"

"I can still play football . . ."

"Touch or tackle?" he said, letting his body relax against hers.

"Any way you want it," she continued. Julie toyed with the gown's strap for awhile and then suddenly pulled the bow apart. "And I can go on long, expensive vacations or play Corie Bratter in *Barefoot In The Park*—with good makeup."

Her hand started a slow descent down her body, still clutching the sheer fabric. The gown moved with her hand until inch by inch the top of her newly enlarged breasts became visible and Robert's expression underwent a healthy change for the better.

"And I can cook and I can clean house, and, oh yes," she said sexily, "there's one other thing I forgot to mention."

The nightgown cleared her nipple as Robert bent down to her chest to take it in his mouth.

"Let me guess," he murmured when he came up for air.

The last image to play in Julie's mind before his strong fingers began moving over her was completely out of context to their lovemaking. It was the disapproving face of Dr. Bain. He was looking down at her from above a swirl of flowing white robes. His expression was one of pure worry.

MARCH
The Third Month

9
Danbury, Connecticut

LATER, JULIE WONDERED HOW IT COULD HAVE taken her so long to figure out what was happening.

After shopping in Danbury, the ten-mile journey home was uneventful until she approached the blinking red lights of the train-crossing near Milbrook. Waiting for the train, which was still not visible, Julie let her mind drift toward her baby. It was strange to think that her only other child had been born nearly twenty years earlier. And equally strange that her first marriage now seemed like an old script performed and since forgotten. Like her, TJ had been a struggling actor, although his audiences had been mostly the lunch and dinner crowds at various Manhattan restaurants.

The two of them were all they should have been at twenty-three: romantic, broke and unconscious about life. Casey was the only lasting product of their marriage, and she'd borne most of the scars from the breakup. Of course, there was also Julie's burden of guilt about Casey's devastated childhood. In the small hours while Robert slept soundly next to her, Julie had to confront the fact that Casey's childhood was the most serious failure of her life. She thanked God that in recent years she and Casey had developed a true friendship.

Back in the present again, Julie pressed her belly and tried to feel the new life stirring within, and as soon as she did, not surprisingly, Robert came quickly to mind. Very simply, Robert and the baby were inseparable. Robert was the great love of her life, a love still deepening, and the baby would be the living symbol of that love.

She pictured Robert in his three-piece suit behind the mahogany desk at the agency. She thought about his strong physique, his handsome face and soft-spoken strength. The memory of his scent filled her senses and she felt heat surging through her body. It was amazing how much they still excited each other. She was about to add the words "at their ages" when she felt the gentle, metallic tap on her rear bumper.

The day at the ad agency had been frenzied. Robert knew the highly competitive commercials they were running for San Paulo wine would be controversial, but when the competition filed suit against both the client and the agency, there had been a mad legal scramble to check the research on which the commercial's claims had been based. So far, the lawyers were cautiously optimistic, which said a lot for a group of professionals who were negative, by reflex. It had taken Robert until almost four in the afternoon to close the door, order a sandwich, and reach for the phone to call Julie.

When no one answered, he sat back in the small, glass-and-chrome-decorated office he had designed and pushed aside his first thought: "something's wrong."

Julie's maternal announcement had caught him dumbfounded, but afterwards, his anticipation grew almost daily. When in the past he'd thought about becoming a father, it had seemed a remote, abstract idea. Like Julie, he had been married once before, but there'd been no children. Before his wife of eleven years was taken from him in the auto accident, they had been uncommonly happy, but neither had felt the nesting urge for a larger family. After Ann's death he was alone again until his mid-forties, and during that bleak, lonely time he'd channeled his energies into a business that now boasted sixteen employees and a six-figure profit. But the agency had never replaced the deep need that Julie had come along, miraculously, to fill.

Again he dialed their number. When she still didn't answer he reached for her picture on the desk and turned it until it faced him. After his first marriage had ended, he'd never believed consoling friends who said he would find someone else. Even when he'd met Julie he hadn't been ready to accept the possibility that his life was about to undergo such a dramatic change for the better. Which wasn't to say he hadn't instantly found her attractive—in many ways. From the start Julie had seemed *right,* and her picture on his desk captured some of that rightness. She was pretty in a vivacious, impish kind of way, a coyer Jane Fonda. Her features weren't classically beautiful or out of a Wilhelmina Models headsheet, but in his business he'd seen hundreds of models and, honestly, he disdained the striking, often vapid, look of the professionals. Also, Julie was on the small side, just a shade under five feet, three inches. Her real attractiveness, however, came more from the inside. She gave off an aura of energy that was almost hypnotic, and that was something he soon found hard to live without.

Most of all, though he often found her overpowering, he began to realize he could trust her with his private feelings; her support was always there. She was on his side and it was something he hadn't found in a woman since Ann. No matter how paranoid, the thought of harm coming to her was hard to push aside; it was why he reached for the phone one more time. He smiled, suddenly remembering the embarrassment over his perpetual erection during their first months together. Eventually they came to joke about it. Suddenly, he felt the arousal once again, just in time for the lawyers.

The vehicle in the rear-view mirror was a dark blue, late-model van that towered over her Oldsmobile. As soon as it bumped her, Julie adjusted her mirror to get a better view of its driver, but his windshield had a smoky color and she could barely make out a male shape. It was probably a kid who hadn't quite gotten the hang of driving it, yet.

The train whistle diverted her attention. It was still a

good distance away, and for a moment the clatter and whistle reminded her of an appreciative audience. Then she looked back into the mirror. It would have been nice if the driver had at least waved or made some gesture of apology.

She suddenly felt movement in her belly and with an immediate grin cupped her stomach with her hand. At that instant the Olds was bumped—this time sharply—from behind.

After the lawyer called unexpectedly to cancel the meeting, an astonished group of employees watched Robert leave the office a good hour earlier than usual. Two minutes later he was in his car heading north for Route 7, and home. He wasn't worried about anything specific, but he felt worried, nonetheless. His foot on the gas pedal, his heart fluttering uncomfortably, he raced home.

When his worrying spells kicked in, he always had pretty much the same thought: Julie's not very much grounded in reality; she's an artist, flighty and more than likely to go skipping into the wild blue yonder if the possibility presents itself. Ever since he'd met her she'd never seemed alert to the risks of the world, or, if she was, she seemed not to care, as a matter of principle; it was true in the old days in the city, whether a midnight outing in a blizzard to surprise him with cheesecake, or a reckless career move that cost her a role. She still drove at high speed while telling stories, and she still went outside the house looking for crazy people who were trying to harass her. The energy she brought to living might be her greatest

75

attribute, but it could also be her undoing. Robert found his attitude toward her in constant conflict, a balancing act between pressing for her safety and allowing for her independence and high spirits.

In the failing light of the bleak winter evening, Robert concentrated on the road ahead. He assumed it was the heater that produced the small drops of perspiration on his forehead. He ignored the tremor in his chest. He also decided the speedometer would have to be checked the next time the car was in the shop. The needle was pointing to an absurd seventy-six.

At the second bump, Julie jerked her head around angrily.

"What do you think you're doing?" she yelled through the rear window.

Again she waited for a response from the van, and again none came.

She tried to make out a face behind the smoky-gray windshield glass, but couldn't. The shadowy silhouette just sat there, looking straight ahead; she could *feel* eyes staring down at her. Then she thought of the spiders, and an icy chill shuddered down her back. Suddenly her breaths were coming shallow and rapid and she felt her heart thump sharply in her chest. She knew she had to get out of the Olds. Then, as she reached for the door, the van's engine revved up to a scream and its bright lights snapped on.

There was only one road that led into Milbrook off Route 7 and Robert swung onto it, managed to pass an agonizingly slow produce truck, and headed for home, three miles distant on Rock Ridge Road. In the distance he could hear the thin whistle of the homebound commuter train that had come from Grand Central Station in New York. Usually he found the sound reassuring, a reminder of homecomings and reunions that went back to his childhood. For some reason today he found that whistle unnerving.

The train, whistle blaring, hurtled down the tracks toward Julie. It didn't stop in Milbrook anymore, and at the speed it was traveling it couldn't have stopped anyway.

The van jumped toward her again. By the time it smashed her taillights she'd managed to jam the shift into park and squeeze both her feet onto the brake pedal. But the Olds was no match for the heavier vehicle and the collision pushed her hood under the signal gate, within inches of the track. Frantic, she looked to her right, through the passenger window, and saw the huge locomotive, now a quarter of a mile away, bearing down on her, shrieking a blood-chilling warning.

The van's engine roared over the sound of the train as it strained to push her car forward. Julie yanked the gearshift into reverse, and tromped on the gas pedal. For a moment the opposing forces stalemated; Julie thought of bailing out of the car, but instantly realized that the second her foot came off the gas pedal, she'd be pushed into the path of the train. Her mind raced incoherently as she felt the wheels under her begin to lose traction on the gravelly roadbed; again she was inching forward.

The train was less than a hundred yards away now, screaming at her to get out of the way. Frozen, like a deer caught in a powerful light, Julie waited for the crash that would end her life.

Robert saw the train, the van, and Julie's Oldsmobile at the same instant, and in the terrible, elongated moment of recognition his foot came off the gas. His logic told him that Julie had stalled and somehow the van was trying to help her. But there was something wrong with that theory. The train was too close for her to still be in the car. As Julie's windshield snapped the warning signal gate, Robert smashed his hand down into the horn, pressed the gas pedal to the floor and took deadly aim at the unknown driver who, in a few seconds, would end everything in his life worth living for.

In the moments before the train would disintegrate her car, Julie slipped into a curious serenity. Convinced she was about to die, she sensed a part of her yielding to the inevitable. It was an immobilizing acceptance that for an instant brought to an end all of her efforts to survive. In this odd quiet she suddenly felt a single, stirring kick of life in her womb. Instantly she snapped back. The will to survive surged, and her mind seized on a last chance for life.

She yanked desperately on the gear shift as the ground beneath her vibrated from the power of the train. For an eternity the shift seemed fused into position and wouldn't yield, then as she looked to her right and stared into the teeth of the giant killing machine only a few dozen yards away, the shift suddenly released and slammed into forward. At the same instant her right foot hammered down on the gas pedal, and the Olds shot ahead and across the tracks, breaking through the far signal gate with a sharp crack as the great engine roared by behind her.

10

Milbrook, Connecticut

SERGEANT SCOTTY MALLOR USHERED ROBERT AND Julie into a brand-new office that still smelled vaguely of poured concrete. The lighting was stark, and the furniture purely functional. It could have been any small-town police headquarters anywhere in America. At four in the afternoon there were two other officers in the small building, a court stenographer, a custodian and a repairman from the Starbrite Canteen Company, who had the soda machine reduced to its essential parts.

The "Sergeant" before Scotty Mallor's name came as a result of the most important collar of his long career in 1981, when he'd shot out the tires of a private jet taxiing down a runway at Danbury Airport in Connecticut's first attempted skyjacking. But his single-handed heroics had been unauthorized, catching State Police and the Governor's office by surprise; so while the newspapers called him a hero, the official reaction—very quietly executed—was a reprimand. The sticky public relations problem was solved by promoting Mallor to the rank of Sergeant, together with the tacit instruction that he should go no higher. The fact that he knew his progress had an upper limit, people said, accounted for the quiet bitterness that seemed to hang around him like a cloud.

This was a follow-up interview by Mallor, after the visit to their home the evening of the incident.

"We're all concerned with what happened to your wife, Mr. Weston . . . "

"Montgomery," Robert interrupted for the second time. "Weston is my wife's professional name."

"Sorry, it's just that her name is so well-known," Mallor said automatically. He placed a ham-sized palm over his chin. "The thing is, we don't know exactly what you want us to do."

Julie had been biding her time. With an age-old antipathy toward bureaucracy, she'd come with low expectations and had not been disappointed. "Very simply," she started, "find out who tried to kill me, that's all. Can you understand why I might want that?"

Mallor was amused, not insulted, by her sarcasm. He was used to the treatment, especially from the wealthy, who often treated police officers like children or morons.

"First I'm threatened at home. Now, this!" Julie's voice rose waveringly and Robert pressed his hand into her own.

Mallor, a good cop, looked into the beautiful actress's eyes with sympathy. He began gently, without rancor. "In the first place, we have no way of knowing whether the person who left the note is the same as the one in the van. In fact, it's likely they weren't the same person."

"What makes you so sure of that?" Robert asked quietly.

"I didn't say we were sure . . . of anything."

"But . . . " Julie started.

"Too many differences between the two incidents," Mallor continued, undaunted. "One time it's some foolish schoolboy prank—the spiders and weird note . . ."

"Addressed to *mommy*," Julie interrupted again, "that's not a prank; that's sick."

"Still," Mallor replied, "it's juvenile, nothing at all like the van thing, and very probably not the same kind of person. Plus, there was no attempt to communicate with you the second time, like the first."

"What about the van?" Robert asked. "It shouldn't be that hard to find, especially in a small town like this."

Mallor smiled his sad smile. "No, Mr. Montgomery, not hard at all. In fact, I know this may come as a shock to you, but we've already found it."

Robert started another question which Mallor stopped with a raised index finger. "Just a second. Let me explain. It was actually a lucky break. There was a drop in water pressure over in New Castle where they have city water, and they traced it back to the aqueduct leading out from the reservoir. They found a late-model, dark blue van plugging up the main pipe about

81

ten feet under the water line. It also matches the description of a van stolen from Southwestern College last week."

"Were there any prints on it? Anything inside?" Robert asked quickly, leaning forward in his chair.

"Nothing so far in the way of usable evidence. We're still checking, but I wouldn't count on finger-prints. As I mentioned, the van was stolen from a college. It belonged to a fraternity house and must have been driven by dozens of different kids. Given that, and the water, getting good fingerprints looks pretty hopeless."

"What's next?"

Mallor sighed and shook his head. "We've checked out that neighborhood kid you told us about and he was in school the afternoon the note was left. The van is probably going to be a dead end, and as far as the first note goes," he shrugged his shoulders, "frankly, I just don't see the connection."

"I think I do, Sergeant," Robert said, "and I think I can prove it, at least circumstantially." He paused as Mallor nodded, then went on. "Something else hap-pened at the train crossing you haven't heard about."

Mallor's eyes flickered with sudden interest and for the first time Robert realized that despite the officer's phlegmatic demeanor, he sincerely wanted to help them. The realization was sudden and intuitive, and Robert trusted it. He turned to Julie. "Right near the end, when the train was almost on you, what did you do?"

Julie didn't know what he was getting at but tried to remember anything that might be important.

"I told you, I put it into forward gear and stepped on the gas."

"Not that part—before. What happened before you were able to get the car moving?"

"I don't know what you mean. It was in reverse, before that."

"It was hard getting it to move from one gear to the other, didn't you tell me that?"

"Yes. At first I didn't think I could get it out of gear at all."

"And how did you finally do it?"

Whatever Robert's point, he seemed to know where he was going, and Julie tried hard to visualize it again. "I just kept pulling on the shift, the way I had been. Is that what you mean?"

"Did you do anything different, like use two hands, all of a sudden? Anything that increased your strength?"

She thought about it. "No, I don't think so. I was already pulling as hard as I could. The extra adrenaline might have given me . . . " Her words trailed off in a sudden realization. "Wait a minute. I remember feeling the pressure let up. For no reason!"

"Are you sure?" Mallor immediately asked. He seemed to be getting the drift of Robert's reasoning.

"Yes, because one moment the shift was stuck in gear, I guess from the force of the van pushing from behind, and then it was as though the pressure was gone. Moving the gear from reverse to forward was suddenly easy."

Robert turned to the sergeant. "That confirms the same thing I remembered, afterward."

"Which is?"

"When I saw what was happening, I decided the only thing I could do was go for the van. Christ, I didn't even think that would do any good, but it was all I could do."

Julie stared at Robert, trying to imagine what it must have been like for him to watch the train bearing down on her.

"I was probably doing around forty by the time I got close, don't know for sure, but before I could smash the van I suddenly saw its lights go on."

"So did I," Julie broke in, "right before the last bump."

"Not the headlights; I'm talking about the backup lights. For some reason that van started backing up right before the train got there. The point is, he backed away right before he could finish what he started."

Mallor thought quickly and waved off the suggestion. "He saw you headed for him and got scared."

"Impossible. I was coming at him at a blind angle. He couldn't have seen me in his mirror. And he couldn't have heard my horn because of the train whistle."

"So the van backed up at the last minute. He probably thought he'd pushed the car out far enough and decided to take off before the wreck."

"I don't think so," Robert said. "I think the van backed up because whoever was driving knew all along he was *going* to back up. It wasn't because I was coming or because he thought he'd taken care of my wife. It was because he didn't want her to get hit in the first place."

Mallor shook his head. "You're saying it was just a scare?"

Julie stared at the sergeant, feeling the blood drain from her face.

"Yes. And the house incident was a scare too, just a different kind. This guy's intent was to frighten Julie, only he cut it too close." Robert leaned forward toward Mallor again, clenched fists resting on the coffee table between them. "I think the same guy did both things. I just have this powerful feeling about it."

"We tend not to rely on that kind of feeling in my business," Mallor said, "but still, you may be right. If you are, we've got a maniac out there." Mallor stood up and turned toward Julie. "Mrs. Montgomery, I'll do everything in my power to get this guy." Awkwardly, the sergeant put his hand on Julie's slumped shoulder. "I know how hard this must be for you. Try not to worry." He hesitated momentarily, then added, "And please be careful, very careful."

11
Woodbury, Connecticut

NEXT TO THE WINDOW THE INDOOR-OUTDOOR THERMometer read 82 degrees and 24 degrees. The cautious man pulled aside a lace curtain, pressed his cheek to the frosty window glass and looked outside. Straight ahead two high runways of snow edged freshly shoveled slatestone that ran from the front porch down to the country road. The weather forecast had been right and after snowing all night it was about to come down heavily again.

Though it might have been wiser, he would not be deterred from his daily constitutional. With the help of his cane, the path would present no major obstacles, and he could be back well before the new storm struck. But, before he could get out, there would be the usual battle. He moved toward the foyer and, as if on cue, Mrs. Brennan appeared in the front hall, hands on hips, disapproval written on her broad features.

Twenty minutes later, the master of the house appeared at the doorway of 36 Cabot Lane in an oversized blue-down parka, the kind much younger people usually wore, pile-lined boots, two mufflers and a knit cap pulled over his ears and half his face. A minute or so later, when his boots touched the mixture of sand and snow on the road's surface, Mary Brennan's scowling face finally disappeared from the living room window. Undaunted, the man pressed the cane along his right leg, tightened the knot of the outside muffler with a left hand that no longer worked as well as it once had, and began his deliberate trek toward town.

The move to Woodbury had been a good idea, he thought again as he plodded toward an ancient three-story building he could just make out ahead. The pre-Revolutionary Connecticut town was one of the last unspoiled hamlets in the rolling upstate area. Also, the village people had been kind to him, more so in recent years as they had grown less suspicious, accepting him for what he so obviously was: a kindly, somewhat doddering senior they saw every morning wending his way from his mansion on the hill to Canfield's Pharmacy, where he bought and read a copy of *The New York Times,* as well as the local *Republican Guardian Herald.*

The morning walk was an integral part of his self-prescribed survival plan and one of the main reasons he hadn't been condemned to a wheelchair years before. One didn't have to be a doctor to know that the day a person stopped forcing the machine to function it would inevitably wither. Now, in the wake of years of sickness and hospitalization, he still had a good right arm, and two serviceable legs, could still walk and drive a car, and could still tell nurse Mary Brennan where to get off.

When he arrived at the town's main intersection, the wind was swirling the fallen snow and he felt bone-cold. The driver of a firewood truck waited patiently for him to cross the street, then looked after as he drove by, shaking his head in admiration. Carefully, the old man made his way up the three front steps of the faded-green building, turned the old-fashioned door latch and stepped into Canfield's with a sense of accomplishment—and a brief coughing spell. He sat down on one of the old upholstered red stools with half the gold tacks missing and loosened his muffler in time for the black coffee, which was delivered by Henry Oslow without need of an order. Henry, his junior by only a few years, spoke only long enough to note how he looked, how much snow had fallen the night before and how bad business was. Comfortable things. His newspapers appeared then, and Henry began the half-hour vow of silence that allowed for the older man's perusal of the papers.

It wasn't until the clouds had turned ominous that the old man spotted the article in the *Guardian*. It was the picture that stopped him. She was a pretty woman, past the first bloom of youth, and the focus of the story. Something about her face was familiar and he squinted carefully at the small type through the lower section of his bifocals.

"Local Actress Bumped," the picture caption read. The rest of the article, which appeared in the entertainment section of the paper, was short and written in the semi-literate style adopted by small papers from their big-city counterparts:

"No, we're not talking about getting booted off a picture. This is the real thing. Milbrook's own Julie Weston had a bad scare when someone tried to push her car into the 5:05 from New York at the village's old train station crossing. This reporter also learned that Julie was harassed earlier this year at her home. We hope and pray that the creep responsible for bothering our Julie gets what's coming to him. And more!"

The old man looked up from the paper and stared into an aged amber mirror behind the counter. Something about the picture of the woman was stirring a memory, and he worked to bring it into focus.

When it came to him, he considered it briefly, then quickly tried to dismiss it from his mind. The possibility was just too remote, the product of a bored curmudgeon's tired mind.

He pushed himself up from the stool and forced his body to move toward the door. He did not acknowledge Henry Oslow's wave, as was his custom, nor did he latch the door once he left.

Looking after him with concern, Henry noted that his customer and friend had even forgotten to tighten his muffler against the biting cold. Silent as night, he simply shuffled out into the thick blowing snow of a late winter's day and disappeared.

APRIL
The Fourth Month

12
Milbrook, Connecticut

JULIE HUNG UP AFTER THE LENGTHY CALL FROM LOS Angeles. It was sweet of Stephen Weisberg, her producer, to call, but his greeting had contained an ulterior motive. He'd bid successfully on an exciting new script and wanted Julie to co-star with Nick Nolte, who had already agreed.

Her bittersweet refusal stunned Stephen, who had actually groaned when she'd told him that she was having a baby. It was the first time she'd been confronted with the reality of what the baby would mean to her professionally.

Later, Julie's disappointment dissolved in thoughts of pleasure about the baby, and the new life it would mean for Robert and her.

In the afternoon, wearing a new dress that tented over her, Julie drove through the melting snow to Dr. Bain's office in Danbury. It was the beginning of her fourth month, and this time the consultation was to last about double that of the previous visit.

As he'd done every time, Bain wrapped the black tube around her left arm and tightened it until she felt as if there couldn't be any blood left in her arm. She tried to think her blood pressure down, a mind-over-matter trick she knew was theoretically possible from long-ago lessons in biofeedback. But from the look on Bain's face she still needed a lot more practice.

"Not good, Julie," he said sternly. "As a matter of fact, bad."

Bain was close to sixty and very adept at manipulating his patients. There was, sometimes, a preachy quality in his manner, yet he was lovable enough to get away with it.

"How bad is bad?" Julie asked, knowing Bain often cried wolf as a warning tactic; but the expression still on his face told her this time it simply wasn't the case.

"Let me put it this way. When you saw me the first time your blood pressure was slightly high. I presumed that wasn't unusual for you. The second and third time you were higher still. And now, after treatment no less, the decrease is so little it's really insignificant. In just under four months you've gone up almost a dozen points." He scratched the white stubble of a badly shaved chin and for a moment looked cross. "I'm worried, Julie. This could get serious and we're going to have to treat it as though it's going to get worse."

"But I thought you just said my pressure decreased from last time. Isn't that a sign that we're getting it under control?"

Bain shook his head emphatically. "All pregnant women experience a fall in blood pressure in the middle trimester which you're now in, but your decrease is so slight it might as well be another rise. Do you understand?"

She did. Bain had told her what could happen in graphic detail on a previous visit. If her blood pressure kept going up, there was a real chance of developing something called superimposed pre-eclampsia, an extreme case of hypertension disease with edema and other complicating conditions. From there, further elevation of blood pressure could result in acute toxemia, and, finally, eclampsia itself with convulsions and coma both distinct possibilities.

It could mean not only the end of her baby, but of her. What made it so dangerous was that even a normal case of high blood pressure had to be guarded against with mothers over thirty-five, let alone the kind of readings toward which she might be heading. If it worsened, the only possible solution was abortion, and even that unthinkable solution was slipping away with time.

"Okay, we've got a problem," she sighed. "Just for curiosity's sake, how many women get high blood pressure in pregnancy?"

"Four to seven percent," Bain answered, "that's all."

"And I'm one of the lucky ones, huh?"

"Well, you do understand that you didn't get it in pregnancy, you *brought* it with you. Pregnancy just heightened a pre-existing condition which you must have known about before this. Like during the first pregnancy?"

"I guess so, but the first time was twenty years ago when I was a lot stronger, and I guess a lot calmer. Wouldn't that make a difference?"

"Naturally."

"Also I was a real sixties' health nut and . . . ah, life didn't have some of its more exotic pressures." She thought about the scares of the last few months, which by then Bain knew all about, and decided that exotic was the perfect word.

"Pressure of any kind is against you," Bain said sympathetically," and diet is going to be one of the antidotes."

"Easy on the salt, right? What else?"

"Don't dismiss the salt diet so easily. We still think salt is probably a major threat to some people with high blood pressure, so much so, there's a chance you may even have to be hospitalized before you're done, just because of salt."

Julie braced instinctively as Bain went on.

"No matter how careful you try to be, we live in a world that puts salt into everything, and to people like you, at this time in your life, even a little can be a lot. So if your hypertension gets worse, the only place you can be guaranteed a salt-free diet is in a hospital."

"Isn't that a bit . . . extreme?"

"Not as extreme as what can happen if we can't overcome this thing."

"I see what you mean," Julie said quietly.

"Besides salt intake, overall diet is important, too. The higher your weight, the higher your blood pressure. Obviously. So far you're only moderately above our three-pounds-a-month limit, but it would be better in your case to keep the entire gain under twenty pounds for the full term."

It sounded like a lot to ask. When she had Casey,

she'd gained twenty-eight pounds exactly, much of it in the late part of the pregnancy.

"Of course, if your weight rises a lot, suddenly, say over a pound in a given week, we've got even bigger troubles. That would indicate the start of toxemia, and it can happen any time after the twentieth week."

"Dr. Bain," Julie began formally, "there's nothing more important to me than having a healthy baby, and I know the risk my blood pressure is putting on that. I want you to know that I take everything you've said very seriously. It's been a . . . very difficult time for me."

"All right, Julie," Bain said softly. "I know you understand what's going on. Actually, I'm a bit less worried than, perhaps, I sounded, because deep down I believe we can control your problem as long as we're careful."

Julie smiled immediately. "That's a relief to hear."

"But let's do everything we're supposed to, okay? You've got a strict salt-free diet to follow, as well as your limited caloric intake. There are all the normal restrictions on the list I gave you the first visit. All of it is more important now."

Julie nodded. "Right."

"You'll take your diuretic every twelve days and your potassium pills on exact schedule. Same with the vitamins and iron. And your antihypertensive drug. Possibly we'll increase the dosage next time. Let's see what happens when we do everything exactly right, first. And just as important, if you feel the slightest bit tired or dizzy get into bed right away and stay there."

"Aside from the dizzy spell I haven't really felt very tired. Is that unusual?"

Bain looked at her and smiled a smile that could almost have been described as cute. "For anyone else, yes, it's unusual. For you?" He winked. "Now get dressed."

After she'd finished, Bain returned with one last caution. "The first trimester sets the stage for the rest. It is easier then for any problems you already had to intensify, and they have. The thing to remember now is, with all the medicine we have, and all the knowledge we have, the way you feel up here," and he pointed to her head, "is the most important. I know what you've been through lately and I know how hard that makes it for you to relax."

"How about impossible?"

"You've got to try!" Bain said with uncharacteristic passion. "Maybe we'll have to go to some sedatives. Meanwhile, keep a light schedule and for heaven's sake don't even consider taking on any new projects."

"Promise."

Bain looked at her intently, then finally nodded. "You're dismissed," he said with a sudden twinkle. "And, by the way, just between you and me, I think it's a big loss for Hollywood."

13
New York City

FIFTY-EIGHT-YEAR-OLD ARTIE SHORE SAT AT HIS handsome rolltop desk looking at his own image in the glass of his wife's picture. What he saw was the reflection of a rapidly aging man who, at the moment, looked bored.

After interviewing eight would-be actors during the morning, number nine was waiting to audition in the outer office. For the hundredth time—minimum—he asked himself why he'd stayed in the same musty, memory-filled office in the theater district. The answer, of course, was always the same: Artie hated change. Well, he reminded himself, not *all* change; he fervently hoped that some producer, somewhere, would realize that the world's greatest stand-up comic was currently disguised as a highly successful agent and give him the "big break" he always had been waiting for.

In the meantime, candidate number nine was ready. "Your turn to shine," he crooned, sticking his head into the waiting room and making a grand gesture of welcome to the handsome young actor with the solemn expression.

The young actor came in sounding as if there was a box of marbles jangling in his pocket. He seemed more awestruck than most of the hopefuls who'd preceded him into the wicker chair. At least they'd feigned an air of confidence. A dozen faces played in Artie's mind in place of the youngster's. Wes Calhoun, the great lover. Clair Rheingolde, the injured heroine. Rich Steward, the soap idol. And now, to add to the list of luminaries he'd helped launch, he could proudly add the name Julie Weston. Better late, than never.

He snatched a moment while glancing at the boy's resumé and recalled Julie when she'd first come to him—a skinny kid, cock-sure and scared to death at the same time, with too-little makeup and too much chatter, but he'd spotted the *zetts* right away—that special magic that came along once in a blue moon. Julie was pretty in a guileless sort of way. And unquenchable. She looked nothing like the girl next door, but once you saw her, she made you wish you were the fella next door.

"Okay, kid," Artie blurted out after finishing the brief historical form he made everyone fill out. "As they say in the movies, tell me something about yourself."

"Where should I begin?" the young man answered with a bit too much challenge than suited Artie.

"Well, you've come in without a headsheet, and so far, from your resumé, I can see you were real big on the stage—the high school auditorium stage, that is. You've done some commercials, which I don't hold against you, believe me, and you want to be in the movies." Artie slapped the desk abruptly and held out his hand, palm up. "Congratulations. Shall I call Cecil B. and tell him to set up a screen test?"

Artie waited for a laugh that didn't come, and sighed loudly. Not for the first time he admonished himself for continuing his "tradition" of spending one day a week with his door open to anyone who cared for an audience. He was the *only* agent to still do it. Change, he thought. God, how I hate it. It was a character flaw, he knew, but that didn't help a helluva lot.

Suddenly he wished the interview was over; he'd had enough today and this kid was testing his legendary patience. I'm getting old, he thought, and, with a smile, he wondered if any of his old friends would ever remember that he was sixty-four, not fifty-eight, and if they did, whether they'd keep their mouths shut.

Artie sat back in his old swivel chair and swiveled.

"Anything else you can tell me, lad? Other experience? Do you dance as well as crack jokes?"

"No. I don't dance," the young man said evenly. "I don't like dancing."

"Perhaps you sing? You're voice-trained and sound like Caruso, maybe?" Artie wondered whether his sarcasm was going too far; he didn't like to hurt *anyone's* feelings, but this kid just wasn't trying. At all.

"I don't sing," the kid answered, his tone even and precise.

"Listen," Artie said, gently, "I'm not trying to be rough on you, but I'm a pussycat compared to the people out there you're gonna have to bump into.

101

Personally, I like your look. You're a nice-looking kid.
You got strength and intelligence."

"Thank you," the kid said, without inflection.

"But the world is full of strong, smart, good-looking
kids, and they're all in show business. Have you got
anything else to recommend you, something I can
show other people to make you stick out in their
minds?"

The young man's face relaxed, and, wonder of won-
ders, a thin smile suddenly appeared. He lifted a
briefcase to his lap, opened it and handed Artie a video
cassette.

"Have you got a video player?" the kid asked.

"Does a waiter come with a check?"

The kid didn't laugh and again Artie sighed. "Tell
me, are there actually pictures of you on this?"

The young man nodded.

Artie got up and wheeled a cart with his video
equipment next to his desk. In a minute he got the
machine going and pulled his chair around so he could
sit next to the actor and watch the television screen.

"Aren't you going to turn out the lights?"

"Sure thing," Artie said, thinking: please God, let
this be over soon.

The visuals were a long time coming, and when the
first images finally appeared Artie stared in surprise at
the screen. What he was seeing looked familiar, too
familiar. For a few seconds he couldn't remember, and
then suddenly he was looking at Julie Weston—his
Julie. She was leaving a brownstone in Greenwich
Village and hailing a cab. It was the opening scene

from her last movie, *Larrou,* the film which had recently catapulted her career so dramatically. The titles came up over the action to announce the names of the stars and at that point Artie Shore finally ran out of patience. He spun toward the kid, knowing with certainty, now, that this actor had even fewer cards in the deck than the norm—which was not saying a helluva lot—but before he could say anything, the long, cold blade of a hunting knife pierced his chest and pushed through his lung into his heart.

14
Milbrook, Connecticut

THE OFFICER WHO PHONED THE AD AGENCY ON THE afternoon Artie was killed identified himself as Melvyn Pierce, detective, Manhattan Midtown, New York City. When Detective Pierce told Robert that the murder was probably connected with Julie, he felt a cold fear begin to gather in his stomach. He asked Pierce about the tie-in; however, the detective refused to discuss it over the phone. He had already been in touch with the Milbrook Police and they would escort Robert and Julie to New York the next day, assuming that was convenient, which he very much hoped it would be.

On the way home to break the news to Julie, Robert reviewed the last and most sobering piece of information the detective had told him: a twenty-four-hour police guard would be posted outside their home.

As he approached home, the idea of the murder and its implications for Julie made Robert actually feel physically weak, as though the energy that was such a normal part of him had simply dissipated with the flick of a switch. Having known Artie, how kind he was, how incapable of hurting anyone, made his murder seem all the more ghoulish and incomprehensible.

Robert paused for a moment in the car after pulling into the drive, searching futilely for words that might cushion the blow for Julie. Before he could get out of his car, a Milbrook police car pulled sharply in behind him.

He saw Julie appear at the door, then step out onto the front porch.

Robert sighed heavily and hoisted himself out of the car. "What's going on?" Julie called from the porch, worry in her voice.

"A nightmare," Robert said softly to himself, then, for Julie, he called, "Hold on a minute, I'll be right in."

"Is everything all right?" she shouted.

Robert stared up at her and their eyes seemed to lock in instant understanding. He shook his head slowly back and forth, and repeated, "I'll be right in."

"Robert Montgomery," he said, reaching out to take the young, blond, police officer's hand. "I appreciate your being here."

"Patrolman Moundsey," the officer responded.

"Sorry this is necessary. I'll need a list of people you might expect here in the next few days, and their license plate numbers."

"Of course," Robert answered, surprised at how calm his voice sounded. "I have to inform my wife of what's happened, then we'll get you the information you need."

"Fine, Mr. Montgomery. I'll be here." The young cop moved back to the patrol car, shoes squeaking softly.

Robert gathered himself up and walked to the house, aware of Julie watching him from the living room window. With a certainty he'd rarely felt before in his life, Robert knew when he finally entered the house that a part of Julie, perhaps a vital part, would be changed forever.

He took her in his arms the moment he was through the door. "I have some terrible news," he heard himself saying as if in a dream, and watched as her eyes went wide with alarm. She took her hands off him to clutch her shoulders protectively, stepping back as she did. It hurt him just to look at her.

"It's Artie," he said, "the police just called me."

Julie didn't move, did not react.

"He was found murdered this morning. In his office."

A soft whimper escaped Julie's lips.

"They don't know who did it, maybe a thief." Robert moved toward her, but Julie backed away.

"Artie?" she said.

Robert nodded, knowing nothing to say that would help.

"Artie," she murmured again, then all of a sudden threw herself into her husband's arms, gripping him fiercely around the back. He stroked her hair as she clung to him, letting her tears come. After a few silent minutes the tears abated and Julie stepped away from him to wipe her eyes and nose.

"It's got something to do with me, doesn't it?" she asked mournfully, devastation plain in her voice.

Robert met her gaze but did not answer.

"That's why the cop is out there, isn't it?"

Robert nodded, then reached for her once again and they clung to one another, saying nothing.

Later, Robert told her what little he'd learned.

"And they think whoever did this to Artie is the same one who's been after me?" Julie asked quietly.

"No, they don't know that, but there's some connection. That's why we have to go into the city tomorrow." He kissed her tenderly, and again she broke down. When she calmed, she was pale and weak.

"He was the sweetest man I've ever known. Why would anyone want to hurt him?"

She looked at Robert so sorrowfully it made it hard to fight back his own emotions, but now she needed his strength more than ever. He helped her up and gently rocked her in his arms. They held onto each other for a long time.

"I'm not going to let anything happen to you," he said later. "I give you my word."

"To us," she said, looking at her stomach.

She turned away and stared out the front window. She looked past the railing of the patio to a still dormant landscape that no longer seemed so well-ordered and eternal.

"You know, Robert," she said with a flash of intensity, "for the first time in my life I think *I* could actually kill somebody."

Then Julie began to cry again.

15
New York City

NYPD DETECTIVE MELVYN PIERCE WAS A MAN OF few words, none of them judgmental, and all of them business. He was in his mid-thirties, a young man to have achieved such high rank, but despite his youthfulness his manner was polished and decisive. Recently transferred to Midtown from a Brooklyn precinct, he was a by-the-book cop who was impatient of deviation from procedure. Standard procedure was slow, Pierce knew, often ponderously slow, but it was also thorough and complete, which more often than not brought the relevant facts of a case to light. He was a young cop, but a traditional one all the same and even those who assailed his rigid personal manner behind his back admitted that he was good at what he did.

Pierce had a battery of questions about Julie's relationship with Artie and his other friends, and he pressed hard for information about her recent surprise party which Artie had hosted. He said he'd be sharing his findings with the Connecticut police who'd told him about Julie's other problems. It became apparent in his questions that he was interested in developing theatrical leads, and when Julie asked why, the detective finally came around to the important topic.

"The way in which Mr. Shore was attacked shows the work of someone with," he paused, "let's say, a flair for the dramatic."

Julie stiffened, and said nothing.

"Mr. Shore's body was discovered by a young actress who had an appointment with him at two-thirty. She came to his office on time and waited outside, since his door was closed, and since Mr. Shore's secretary had the day off. Sometime after three, the actress opened his office door and found Mr. Shore lying between two chairs. He was alone and already dead."

Julie stared intently at Pierce, trying to control herself. He looked back at her directly and she thought she'd never seen such expressionless eyes in her life. They seemed like mirrors, reflecting the misery and sadness all around him.

"The room was dark," Pierce continued, "except for the television screen. A video tape had been shown but was finished, so the screen had only interference on it. The actress heard the interference, and that's why she eventually opened the door."

Pierce handed Julie a video cassette in its sleeve. "This was what had been played."

She handled it carefully, as though it contained something toxic or explosive.

"It's been dusted for prints, and the only ones on it were Mr. Shore's. Can you tell me anything about it?"

"I don't understand how I possibly could . . ."

"Why don't you open it first," Pierce suggested gently.

Julie pulled out the tape, looked at the title, and groaned aloud. She looked up at Pierce, who was standing. "It's *Larrou,* my last film."

"Do you know what Mr. Shore could have been doing with it?"

"I have no idea."

"Was there any reason, any reason at all, that you could think of, for him screening it now?" Julie shook her head as he spoke, but still he continued. "Maybe showing it to an actor for instruction or to a producer or director, say to get you another part?"

"No, I doubt that very much. It's not the way Artie worked. He evaluated; he didn't instruct. And as far as another part for me, I've left the business for awhile. To have a baby."

"Did Mr. Shore know that?" Pierce asked immediately.

"Of course. He was very supportive of my decision."

For a second she thought Pierce looked at her strangely. Then he got out of his chair, reached for the tape and popped it into the cassette player.

"What's this about?" Robert asked. "We've all seen it before. Many times."

"Not this version," Pierce said.

He waited until the interference kicked off, followed instantly by a blank screen which indicated the tape's leader was running. He was still standing while Julie and Robert sat, his arms crossed as though blocking someone's way.

"Right now it appears whoever killed Mr. Shore came with this film and was watching it with him, probably at the time he committed the murder."

"How do you know he came with it?" Robert interrupted.

"You'll see in a minute. Then the killer ran out, leaving the tape deck running. Again, probably on purpose."

"On purpose," Julie repeated. "You mean he wanted someone to find the film? Wanted the police to find it?"

"Not exactly, Mrs. Montgomery. Not the police."

It dawned on her what he was getting at and she slumped down in her seat, her heart beating rapidly.

"Oh God," she said, "they wanted me to see it?"

"I'm afraid so," Pierce said softly.

Robert's hand went out to her and she gripped it tightly.

"The message is not a very subtle one," Pierce added, "although the route he took was devious. In any case I'd like to run the film now, but first I have one more question. Does the name *Tommy* mean anything to you, Mrs. Montgomery? In connection with Mr. Shore, or you in general?"

"Just Tommy?"

Pierce nodded. "Think carefully. Someone Mr. Shore may have known or done business with, or a friend of yours who may have known him. A nickname, even a woman's nickname, maybe?"

The trouble was there were no Tommys she could connect to Artie, and too many she knew, herself. There was Tom Bowen, the director on her last film; Thomas Arbrige, her dance coach whom she hadn't seen in years. Back in Hollywood there was Tomas Rodriquiz, the kid who drove her limo to and from the last shoot. Even the slow Gillick kid up the block from them was named Tom. Then the face of another Tom that should have been the first to come to mind loomed in her memory. Julie let out a long sigh.

"Well, this has nothing to do with Artie, but if the murderer is trying to get to me again, I guess there's one Tommy who might come into this."

"Who's that?" Pierce asked.

"Thomas Jaison."

The name registered on Robert's face and he grimaced imperceptibly. It was a name, he knew, that had caused Julie a great deal of pain.

"Thomas Jaison is my ex-husband. TJ. I never called him Tommy, but he used it quite a bit."

"Can you tell us how to get in touch with him?"

Julie nodded. "Yes, of course."

"All right," Pierce said, "let's run the film, now."

Suddenly the TV screen was filled with shots of a country estate. Julie remembered the scene well. In the movie, she was being stalked by someone lurking in the forest. She instantly remembered the end of the action and had a terrorizing thought.

"He must have deliberately chosen this scene," she said excitedly. "It's not that important to the movie,

111

but it's close to the setting of our own house in Milbrook.''

"The bastard has really thought this out!" Robert added.

As the action progressed, Pierce said they had previously run the whole film for clues. He also said something about an edit the killer must have done himself. While he was speaking, the image of a close-up of Julie, looking afraid, suddenly broke up into the jagged black and white image of torn film. That was followed by a slide that had evidently been shot on cheaper, grainier video tape and spliced to the film's footage. When the slide came clear, Julie read what was there, then fled toward the door holding a hand to her mouth. Robert jumped up and followed her and with both of them out of the room, Pierce continued to stare at the screen.

The message contained in the slide was in white type on a black background. For gruesome effect a few drops of red had been splattered here and there around the message. The words were simple:

> ARTIE'S GONE
> NEXT COMES TOMMY.
> WHO KNOWS WHEN
> I'LL COME FOR
> M-O-M-M-Y!!

16
Wilton, Connecticut

AS THE MOMENT DREW CLOSER HIS HAND CLOSED tightly around the bottle of pills. He tapped the container against the floor and it made the sound of small, hard candies in a cardboard box. He could feel his blood heating and coursing through his body, the tingle of anticipation building at the base of his neck and back. Yet he lay on the floor without moving, focusing entirely on the twenty-five square inches of a bright Sony Trinitron color television set.

The feeling hadn't come as a surprise. It had been growing ever since he'd seen the name of Julie Weston in the newspaper listings two days earlier. Now he was within minutes of his first close-up look at her, closer than on the afternoon he'd seen her coming out of her shower in the house. Closer than at the railroad tracks. Soon her image would be even clearer than in the photographs he had taken from their family album.

For an instant he remembered how one photo had shaken him, and how he'd calmed only after cutting away and burning the part where she was holding the little girl. The little girl was much bigger now and was called Casey.

What about me? the voice shouted from somewhere.

For a moment he felt the Cyclone starting up again, the slow, regular clanking of the cable chain that towed it up the big hill; but he was able to force the sound back until it was only an undertone. The awards ceremony was progressing to her category, and he would not allow himself to be distracted. Not even by the Cyclone.

Being able to see her was a sign, he decided, a prophecy. He put all the curses he knew into one sentence and added her name at the end.

He thought of the two of them, his parents, sitting downstairs with that tiresome, worried look on their faces. Since he'd found the letter he'd begun to hate them for their part in the deception. Now in a moment, they'd see her on the program, too, and the irony of it would be another outrage to his sense of justice. He wondered if they even knew who she was, though that didn't really matter.

His eyes were riveted on the center of the picture. The great honor had been given to Clint Eastwood and some actress he'd never heard of. There were five contenders in her category, the contest of Best Supporting Actress. She'd been nominated for *Larrou,* a film with which he was very familiar. He'd gotten his personal copy months earlier, and had passed it on to Artie Shore.

His breaths were coming in short bursts by the time Eastwood spoke. Then, quickly, the list of nominees

114

came, and when, finally, her name was said, his heart felt as if it were going to burst through his chest. Next, they showed a scene from her movie, a part past where he'd done his editing, and although he knew the scene well, he watched again with perfect fascination. She was cunning as an actress, ugly and cunning. No one but he knew the kind of person she really was, someone capable of the sickest crime of all.

Eastwood opened the envelope that contained the winner's name.

Let her win, he prayed.

Eastwood fumbled with the card inside.

Give the Bitch Goddess one last moment in the spotlight. Give her more to lose when it's time to lose all.

"For best actress in a supporting role . . . the winner is . . . here it comes, folks . . . Julie Weston for *Larrou*."

Watching from his dark room three thousand miles away, he felt electric current passing through his arms. The theater erupted into cheers and applause, and the camera quickly panned wide in a search for the newest Oscar winner. He was the eye of the camera and it finally came to rest on a long shot of a woman in a loose-fitting, lacy gown who was skipping—skipping!—down the great aisle toward the stage.

"Get closer," he yelled out loud, oblivious to the disturbance he was creating in the small upstairs room. He pounded the floor hard with his fist, and as if by his initiation, the camera shot suddenly tightened to her head and shoulders. Then, the moment she reached

115

the dais and turned to face a cheering audience, the image zoomed up and he was inches away from a life-size close-up of her face.

When his eyes went wild in disbelief he was already panting like an overheated animal. She was even more grotesque than in the film. Her long, silken, reddish-brown hair was pulled back at the sides and caught up in a knot above her head. For a second he imagined the hair coming down in two long strands, encircling her neck and strangling her. The effect of her makeup was absurd. The shading and shaping of the planes of her face made her demonically evil, and the result was so powerful he could not turn away. There was a smear of color not her own near the rise of her small cheek-bones, and like the deep shadows on her eyelids and the lipstick painted on her lips, it made her witch-like. The lipstick was cherry-red like her blood and painted tightly, fiendishly. A few thin, blue veins were visible below her chin, traveling down the whiteness of her long, exposed throat and disappearing into the high bodice of her evening gown. Forcing his eyes lower he could see the swelling mounds of her full breasts that produced a deep cleavage, and he tried to picture the smooth flesh and nipple that he wanted to tear away with his teeth. Everything about her was false and evil. She was arrogance and power. She was selfish and slutty. And she was *Mommy*.

The heat was coming back. The Cyclone was about to start.

She began to speak and he felt the texture of her speech on his skin. Her words felt soft and velvety, an expected deception, and they rattled something in his body down below. He struggled to push the feeling away and hated her all the more for the arousal she'd produced in him.

". . . the many who helped someone they said was too old, couldn't act her way out of a doggie bag, and who certainly couldn't win an Oscar."

She was holding the statue up in the air, triumphant, no longer pretending to be humbled by the award. She was jubilant at the cheers, which came again in wave after wave.

It was her moment, he knew; her show. And the hate poured out of him.

The applause finally began to die down, but instead of leaving the podium she stayed. It was her moment and the Bitch Goddess would not give it up easily.

"And now I have a special announcement," she was saying, facing right into the camera. Her eyes were clouding and all of a sudden she was either nervous or afraid. Now some of the false bravado was gone, and she was having trouble with her words. For a moment her expression showed embarrassment and her cheeks flushed. His mind was spinning in confusion and he had to force his concentration on each of her words.

". . . love you all, but regret telling you I'll be leaving for awhile. But I'll be back, I promise."

It wasn't making any sense. The audience hushed in surprise.

". . . best reason in the world . . ." she said, raising her voice. All at once she moved from behind the dais, and turned to show her rapidly expanding profile. "I'm having a baby!!"

117

The audience almost immediately broke into enthusiastic applause.

Suddenly the picture cut to the audience again and he watched the people rising from their seats. Then the camera came back to her, and the anger mushroomed out of him anew.

He felt the Cyclone chain click one more time and move to the very top of the rise. For a moment the front car hung in suspension, and then it moved forward to start its drop down the big hill. In sudden panic he ripped open the bottle he still clenched in his hand and pushed two green pills into his mouth. A few seconds later, he took another. He swallowed hard, without water, gagging and knowing it would be too long until they began to work. He closed his eyes, but even then the single hateful word lit up on the back of his lids, blinking off and on in neon red. Taunting him. BABY. BABY. He saw her face again, smiling, resplendent and ghastly; he sprang to his feet with a howl.

When his foot went through the television set's screen the Trinitron exploded in a flash of electric light.

The couple downstairs jumped in alarm. On their feet, they stared at one another, fear in their faces. When the screaming began, the husband took his wife's hand, though he could not find the strength to look again into her sad, haunted eyes, before walking to the upstairs bedroom alone.

MAY
The Fifth Month

17
St. Maarten, Dutch Antilles

THE ANXIETY ROSE THIRTY-FIVE THOUSAND FEET with Robert and Julie and traveled from New York to the Caribbean.

In the beginning, the entire focus of her anxiety had been on the reason someone had chosen her. Even after it had become impossible to dismiss the episodes as pranks, she was able to convince herself that her fame was the reason she'd been singled out. But it was the killer's use of the *Mommy* weapon that had finally defeated all of her best attempts to rationalize, leaving her in a state somewhere between continuous weakness and outright panic.

It was a cruel irony, too. Until then, the word had carried such great warmth and new meaning for both Robert and her. Then, all at once, it had come to represent an ultimate, sick evil.

Since *Mommy* had been used on the film at Artie's, Julie seemed to hear or read it everywhere. She nearly went mad trying to figure a connection to her adversary that could account for its use. Was it simply his

121

peculiar kind of sick humor, a word he knew was filled with paradox because it always came with a threat? Or because he'd known all along that she was pregnant?

Worst of all was the thought that he was so crazy that no pattern to his actions could ever be discerned. His own craziness could be an antidote, a deterrent to the logic that was Pierce and Mallor's best weapon. And, of course, if he was crazy, there was the clear possibility that he was getting worse all the time.

For the first part of the flight Julie was unable to remove her mind from her family and luxuriate in the expectation of St. Maarten. The beginning of May wasn't high season, but after all the things that had happened, getting out of the country for a week was an idea whose time had definitely come. Dr. Bain had given a hearty approval for the week-long vacation, and Casey was safely away from the house at school, so there was no good reason not to go. And although it was already spring in Connecticut, it was still cold enough to enjoy a sudden change to the tropical heat of the Dutch Antilles.

Julie had felt compelled to call TJ before leaving. Once she'd reached him at his L.A. home, it was amazing to see how much emotion was still left. The discovery was in sharp contrast to the empty feeling she remembered so vividly from the divorce proceedings. The police had, of course, already contacted him, but Julie filled in all the specifics and found herself crying all over again when she got to Artie. By the time they were finished they'd both shed tears. Julie ached when she hung up, and found herself weeping again for Artie, for herself, and for a man who, no matter how many years had passed, was still an intimate part of her life.

Talking to TJ was only a bit harder than telling her mother what was happening. At first Julie had wanted to hold everything back from her, but Pierce had pointed out that there was always the chance the twisted mind pursuing Julie would twist in another direction. Then, anyone close to her could conceivably become a target, and certainly a mother wasn't that large a leap.

In fact, of all the killer's potential victims, Mom was clearly the most defenseless. It wouldn't be hard for someone to find her address in Brooklyn where she lived alone with only a doddering old doorman between her and the world outside. Robert had been a dear, suggesting she stay with them in Connecticut, but it was hard to really know if that would actually make her more, or less, safe. For the time being, they tried to convince her to move in with Julie's sister in Philadelphia, but in addition to not wanting to leave her own place, the argument against it was too easy. Mom was quick to point out that it wasn't any safer in Philadelphia; there was no such thing as absolute safety, anywhere. If they could shoot presidents, she posited, what problem would it be to get to one old lady from Brooklyn, no matter where she went?

Pierce had visited her mother, and had ended up agreeing with her. He did have a locksmith change the front-door lock and had advised Julie that her mother was going to have more regular visits from a certain older gentleman with whom she had recently been playing a lot of gin.

The roar of the 747's engines suddenly let up, breaking Julie's thoughts, and she could feel the great plane begin to descend. Then the magical waters of the Caribbean were visible in myriad shades of turquoise, green, and violet. She felt Robert's hand slip into hers.

"Let's do our best to relax," he said. "It's important."

"I know," Julie answered. "I'll try."

"I feel so damn helpless," he said with unexpected intensity.

The idea of a vacation suddenly seemed something close to ludicrous. No matter how perfect the Caribbean weather, they had brought their own clouds with them.

When the locally well-known singer from the Silver Slipper Club called Casey at the dorm to catch a late drink, she put down her Blake and felt her face go flush. This was going to be the night, she decided. She was ready for Jesse Foxboro.

She could already picture herself at the jazz club just off the Wellesley campus and the smoky basement room that seemed to pulse to the bass player's beat. The room was small and warm, and dominated by the smooth, soulful voice of Jesse Foxboro. He was a man she could watch endlessly. It was like being mesmerized by the power of wind. At thirty-five he was still raw and pure, and he did something to her that no man had done before. It was more than the wiry, tightly-

124

muscled frame, and the dark eyes that seemed to hold secrets. He had an inner energy and a confidence that drew her to him like a magnet. Every time he looked at her while he was singing it made her lose her breath, and even thinking about him she could feel herself respond.

Jesse had become her preoccupation, and tonight, if he wanted her, she would be his.

Jesse had come along at the perfect time. Ever since the day Robert had taken her aside and told her about Artie, the danger to her mother had become frighteningly real. Not a day had passed—not even a few hours—when she hadn't wondered what her mother was doing and whether the dorm phone might ring with terrible news. Since then she had called home every night. For the first time she realized how terrible it must have been for her stepfather, who had taken even the earlier "incidents" with deadly seriousness. It made her understand how much she loved her mother. It was a relief that they were safely out of the country for a week.

Casey stood in front of her open closet, staring at a wardrobe that all at once seemed inadequate and immature. She tried to imagine herself in each of the garments, and saw Jesse's long, strong fingers moving over the folds of fabric as he slowly undressed her. After she had showered, she moved to the mirror and examined her body from the side. It was a good body—as she imagined Jesse's to be; it was strong, with each part well-defined. She had inherited a lean build, more from her father than from her mom.

A few minutes later Casey, just ready to leave, got a

shout down the hall announcing a phone call. It was just what she didn't need right now.

Her first inclination was not to take the call, but then she realized it might be Jesse with some last-minute change of plans. She walked quickly down the long hall and took the phone from Nancy Tompkins, who announced that the man at the other end "sounded dreamy."

"This is Casey," she answered. "Who is it?"

"Casey?" the velvety young voice asked.

The single word was all it took to know Jesse wasn't at the other end. At least none of the evening's plans had been changed. The thought made Casey feel generous. Whoever it was, she would give him the brush, but in a nice way.

"Yes, and now it's your turn to identify yourself," she said cheerily.

There was a long pause, and Casey repeated the question, this time with irritability.

"You don't know me," the unperturbed young man began, "but I'm a friend of your mother's."

The voice had more to say, but there was nothing in the rest of the message that required a response from Casey. When the voice stopped, Casey let the phone fall from her hand and just stood there, the color draining from her face. The phone was still swinging under the coin-box when she reached her room and began to frantically empty her handbag. The shaking that had started during the call became almost uncontrollable as she sorted through the bag's contents looking for the piece of paper with the number of the Silver Slipper. In the time it had taken to stumble from the end of the hall to her room she'd been forced to decide she couldn't risk the trip to see Jesse Foxboro.

Not with some maniac out there who said he was "waiting for her" and who kept calling her *sis*.

18
St. Maarten

JULIE AND ROBERT HAD ENJOYED—SOMEHOW—A full day. The sun had been hotter than they'd thought it would be, and by mid-afternoon even the many puffy clouds were not enough to relieve the heat. Julie's well-rounded stomach made walking in the sand harder than normal, and she could already feel herself waddling, which gave Robert endless opportunity for making good-natured sport of her. But she was still at home in the water and pleased that her new and less-than-aerodynamic shape had little effect on her ability to swim. The buoyant water was warm, fragrant and impeccably clear, and once in it she marveled at its restorative powers.

After dinner at the hotel's skytop restaurant, Robert played blackjack at the casino. It was amazing to watch him bet large amounts with such ease and confidence, especially since he displayed no talent whatsoever at the game.

After Robert had lost the first hundred it was followed by a second almost as fast, and finally Julie had to drag him away from the table with a "better offer." Patting his behind surreptitiously, she suggested a game they could both win, and he let himself be convinced. Then, on the way to their room, Julie stopped for a single turn at a huge one-armed bandit, and with two quarters won back half of her mortified husband's losses.

Later, Robert was under sparkling white sheets looking as tan as if he'd been on the beach for several days instead of hours. Julie was still in her gown and reached into the dresser for a folded lace nightgown, the sexiest thing she could find at The Blessed Event Maternity Store in Stamford. She touched the delicate violet ribbon that trimmed the hem of the neck and sleeves. Not bad for a fat suit, she thought. Robert would like it. In fact, Robert seemed to be liking everything, lately. It was hard to know for sure whether he found her as attractive as before, but if his actions were any indication, it was now even more exciting for him. For one thing, there had been a noticeable increase in the frequency of their lovemaking. But it wasn't just the lovemaking. There were more little affectionate things he did. With an inward smile she remembered that having a baby was more of a novelty to him than to her. As she reached for the nightgown she wondered how big she could get and still be attractive.

Julie stepped into the dressing room and closed the door behind her.

"Think you can hang on for another minute?" she taunted from the small room.

"I can if you can," Robert answered.

She knew the evening gown was no longer able to drop over her bulging stomach to the floor, so she went through the more arduous routine of working it up over her head. When she was completely naked she cupped her belly in both hands and, for a second, felt movement. Satisfied, she took hold of the maternity nightgown and let it billow down to the floor; she had both arms through the straps and her head through the neck when she felt the paper receipt against her skin, inside the fabric. At first, she wondered how she'd forgotten to take it out before packing for the trip, and then put it out of her mind. With the gown on, she turned to the mirror and was pleased to see how the material gathered at all the right places. If someone didn't know she was almost five months pregnant, he might not guess from the loose, peasant style of the garment. It was damn sexy, she was quick to allow. Lucky man!

Ready to leave the dressing room, Julie stooped to retrieve the receipt from the carpet and put it on the dressing table. She'd already reached for the light switch when the red writing she'd just seen on the receipt returned to her mind and she stopped cold.

She grabbed the receipt and held it up to the light. The top of the paper quieted her. It *was* the customer copy of the bill from The Blessed Event, and she breathed a sigh of relief. It was only after she had turned the paper over and put it back on the table that she saw the rest of the writing in a red that turned out to be lipstick—her own lipstick. She recognized the scrawl from another time.

> LADYBUG, LADYBUG
> FLY AWAY HOME
> YOUR HOUSE IS ON FIRE
> YOUR CHILDREN WILL BURN

After a frustrating hour, Robert was finally successful in placing two calls. One was to Wellesley, Massachusetts, the other to the St. Maarten Airport.

The first plane out in the morning left just after seven-thirty. It took off in a violent thunderstorm. Julie and Robert were on it.

19
Wellesley, Massachusetts

THE WARY MAN STANDING NEXT TO CASEY WAS A special security officer supplied by Wellesley College. Immediately after the call to the dorm, Casey had reported the threat to both the school authorities and local town police. She had made such an uproar that before finishing, she'd received offers of protection from both. Of course, the fact that her mother was a famous actress hadn't hurt her appeals. The authorities knew there was a chance the episode would hit the papers, and they wanted to appear in the best possible light. For once, Casey appreciated her mother's fame, and had used her name liberally.

Their decision to fly directly to Boston's Logan Airport and not Kennedy in New York was made to save Casey a trip home. They arrived in Boston by early afternoon on what should have been the fourth day of their vacation in St. Maarten.

But when they deplaned and saw Casey with a strange man at the end of the ramp, Julie's reaction was anger, not relief.

"What are you doing here?" she cried so loudly that a number of people turned in their direction. The outburst was quickly followed by an intense but brief embrace after which Julie held Casey at arm's length, shaking her head incredulously.

"The whole point was for you to stay in the dorm. How could you take such a chance by coming here?"

Casey looked more collected than Julie had expected; the reason soon became clear. After a night of thinking about everything that had happened, Casey's terror had turned into anger.

"That little bastard," she said venomously. "He didn't sound any more than sixteen, for Chrissakes."

"He's already killed someone," Julie shot back. "Don't you see why nothing else about him matters, now?"

Casey went quiet and it was only after Robert urged her to go on that she took a deep breath and continued, this time with self-pity in her voice.

"Last night I changed my whole life around because I was afraid. At first I thought I had to, but I didn't like it. Well, I won't do it again." She took hold of her mother's arm and squeezed it. "If we always do what he says, we might as well crawl into a hole and stop living right now." She tossed her head defiantly. "Not me. I won't do it. And I'm not going into hiding."

"That's the stupidest thing . . . " Julie started, then stopped herself, recognizing the same line of reasoning in Casey that she'd used in the beginning, herself. But her own courage had eventually ebbed. It was one thing to be aggressive after being scared, but after Artie's death, her bravery had died, too.

She turned to Robert, looking lost.

"Your mother is right, Casey," he said calmly. "You have every right to feel outraged now, but this isn't the time to take chances. The fact is, this kid is a killer and he *is* able to force us to change our lives. And that's all there is to it."

"It doesn't have to be," Casey replied quickly. She was still defiant, but some of the vehemence was gone.

Robert sensed the change and held out his arm to her.

"Yes it does, honey," he said, gathering her to his chest. "For a while, at least, it does."

Casey looked at her mother. Their eyes were filling with tears.

"I'm so scared," Casey said weakly as they embraced.

"I know, baby," Julie answered, "we all are."

They walked briskly to the car, which was waiting on the inner airport roadway. The bodyguard went first, checked the area, and they got in and quickly pushed down the door locks. But it wasn't until the car was moving freely away from the heavy airport traffic that they had any sense of temporary safety.

The remainder of the afternoon and night was spent in the Carlyle Hotel in Boston proper. The next morning the guard joined them and they drove back to Wellesley. There, they were met by a detective from the small town's police force. After a morning of planning precautions for Casey, which included a promise of constant surveillance on campus, and seeing that she had become more realistic about the danger, Julie and Robert agreed to let her remain at school. The summer break was less than a month away, and then she'd be able to return to the protection of home. In the meanwhile, she'd come home weekends, escorted both ways. When it was time to say good-bye, Julie had to be pulled away from her to begin the long drive back to Milbrook.

In the end Casey was right. No matter what the perils were, life didn't stop.

20
Danbury, Connecticut

THE SHORTNESS OF BREATH AND TINGLING SENSATIONS came on during the night, and when Julie awoke the next morning in a pool of perspiration, the first thing she did was reach for her hypertension pills. The physical symptoms were undoubtedly a delayed reaction to the scares at Wellesley and St. Maarten, as well as in response to two precautions that had greeted her at about eleven o'clock, when they'd arrived home from Boston.

While they'd been away, Robert had arranged for the installation of an elaborate alarm system on both the first and second floors of the house. In addition to an instant relay to the police station five miles away, every door and window had been wired with electrical contacts. Once the contact was broken, a shrill, high-pitched warning tone would sound, followed by a loud bell if the system wasn't shut off within thirty seconds. There were also sonic boxes placed at entrances and exits to all major rooms in case an intruder entered, undetected; any movement in the room would set off the same warning tone and bell.

The second precaution had been more unsettling. After Robert had poured a small brandy to settle Julie's nerves, he'd left the room, returning with a compact, plainly wrapped package. Inside there was a small handgun he'd purchased before their trip, but when he'd tried to give it to her, Julie wouldn't touch it. Without forcing the issue, he'd firmly told her he was going to teach her how to use it. She was to keep it in the bedroom night table on her side; Robert had put it there himself when she'd refused to discuss it further. That was when she'd gotten up and gone to bed, feeling dizzy and nauseous. But later, lying in the dark in the night's stillness, she'd had to admit relief at knowing there was an alarm system in her home and a gun in her drawer.

Casey had arrived home by twelve noon that Friday for a long weekend. Julie had an appointment with Dr.

Bain later in the afternoon and the two of them drove to the doctor's office together. They spent the forty-minute trip looking for phantom vans that never appeared, inching up the same railroad crossing, then speeding across, traveling only the main roads with painstaking care.

Julie's dizziness had persisted all morning, letting up just before her four o'clock appointment. The preceding day, the nurse had called and requested her to drink four glasses of water during the morning and not go to the bathroom; the same nurse greeted her at the office, handing Julie a fifth glass, even before exchanging pleasantries. By then, Julie's bladder was nearly bursting. This seemed to please Bain no end when he personally escorted her into his examination room, leaving Casey to wait with the nurse.

"I have good news, bad news and no news," he offered later, after performing a series of tests that were becoming routine.

"Let's start with the good," Julie said wryly. "I have the feeling I already know the bad."

Bain pressed his hands together. For some reason he was more relaxed than usual. "As a compromise, let's start with the 'no news.' Despite my continuous badgering and complaining to the laboratories, the results of your amniocentesis still aren't ready."

"Okay," Julie said with a hint of disappointment. She thought back to four weeks before when Bain had confirmed what she'd already known, that she needed an amniocentesis because she was over thirty-five. Past that age, the test had become routine. Initially, the thought of having a long needle stuck into her

135

stomach had been frightening, but Bain had managed to put her at ease, and by the time the local anesthetic had taken effect, Julie had to admit the procedure had been almost painless. In only a few seconds, Bain had inserted the needle into the amniotic sac surrounding her baby, and had drawn off a small amount of fluid.

The idea of the test was fascinating. Since the amniotic fluid already contained fetal cells, an analysis of the life within her could be performed with remarkable accuracy. With the technique, it was possible to diagnose with certainty, before birth, almost every known disease caused by defective chromosomes.

"So much for the pull I have around here," Bain was saying. "The results are going to take six to eight weeks, so it's still a bit early."

Julie did some quick math and came up puzzled. "If the test takes that long to be read and it's performed about the sixteenth week, then you wouldn't know until, what, the twenty-second week? That's about five and a half months into it. So if, God forbid, the test does show some abnormality, isn't it a bit late for any . . ." The word came to mind, but she felt uncomfortable about using it. The illegal operation she'd had at the end of her first marriage was something she never wanted to repeat or even think about, again.

"Abortion?" Bain said for her.

She nodded.

"Well, you're right. If we got something tragic from the test, we wouldn't be able to abort, at least not in the normal way. But the odds are so much in our favor there's no point in discussing it now."

Julie smiled gratefully. She also noticed the way he kept saying *our. Our* chances, *our* baby, *our* diet. She was beginning to think he was eventually going to go into labor right along with her. She wondered when it was all over if he'd say *our* stretch marks.

"Now for the bad news," Bain went on, closing the distance between them and becoming stern again. "I want you to tell me why I shouldn't put you into a straightjacket and start feeding you myself."

Julie was taken by surprise.

"Judging from what's happened to your blood pressure, I'm beginning to think I can't trust you to handle it on your own."

"It's bad again?" she asked meekly.

"It's bad still," he replied quickly. "No, it's worse still. You've had a jump at a time when it should be going down. Now I know you've been good about your weight. It's only up a little over two pounds, so we've got to look somewhere else. You tell me."

"Trust me," Julie said. "I've stayed with the diet completely, the salt especially. You scared me enough the last time."

Bain thought for a minute. "Your personal problem, I mean the man . . . is he still . . ."

Julie darkened. "You remember when Robert and I took off for St. Maarten? Well, he threatened my daughter right then."

Bain shifted in his seat, immediately concerned.

"I don't know what to do about it," Julie added, emotion rising in her voice. "If that's what caused my blood pressure to rise, I just don't know what to do."

"I'm very sorry, Julie. This must be unbelievably rough on you."

"It's very difficult," she answered. She thought a moment, then asked, "Could there be any other reason my pressure is going up?"

"I couldn't say for sure. We're really not positive about all the causes of high blood pressure, even today. We don't know why people of equal physiognomies have different pressure readings. We only know for certain that some things can make it worse, salt and overweight, for example. Also, we know we can lower pressure artificially with certain drugs and diuretics. They decrease the volume of blood and the pressure on the vein walls, but there's a problem here, too. Diuretics may have side effects some women can't tolerate, like cramps and dizziness. As a matter of fact, if your dizzy periods continue, we'll have to cut the diuretics back."

Bain stood up and walked to the door of the examination room. Hand on doorknob, he continued, "But even though I'm concerned about your high readings, you still have a way to go before we need to consider real emergency measures. The diet will help more than you think, plus I believe we can put you on some mild sedatives to help you deal with your . . . problem."

Bain opened the door and called to his nurse, then asked Julie, "Perhaps Casey would like to join us for the happier part of our visit."

Julie smiled at another use of "our."

"We're going to take a look at my brand-new computer. And while we're at it, we'll take a look at your new baby, too."

138

"A sonogram?" she guessed, brightening.

"Ultrasonogram," he corrected. "That's why we asked you to drink all that water. Do you think Casey would get a kick out of it?"

"If she doesn't, I'll give *her* a kick."

She moved toward Bain at the door but then stopped and faced him. "I'm worried about the sedatives. Is there any risk to the baby?"

"Julie," Bain said, tilting his head down until he was looking at her over the tops of his wire-rimmed spectacles, "all things considered, the sedatives seem appropriate. But are they a risk? Let me put it this way. Getting up in the morning is a risk; eating food someone else prepared is a risk; walking down a flight of stairs is a risk. Even the doctor you choose to help plan for your baby is a risk. Do you understand what I'm saying?"

"I know what you mean. By the way, can you recommend a good doctor?"

"Flattery will get you nowhere," Bain responded in good humor. "Now how about your first look at the next Montgomery generation?"

By the time Casey had joined them in the new room, Julie was inspecting the ultrasonogram machine. She presumed it would be some amazing-looking piece of industrial engineering, but it turned out to be a rather small unit that looked more like an Apple computer than NASA's space center. Like the amniocentesis, the ultrasonogram hadn't existed when she'd been pregnant with Casey.

Bain introduced them to the young nurse-technician who'd been specially trained on the system, and she began to rattle off the features and capabilities of the computer with the drone of someone who'd done it many times before. Julie was fascinated and hadn't run out of interest when Bain said a demonstration would answer everything. Before she was ready, Bain handed her another full glass of water and explained, "The fuller your bladder, the better the picture," while waiting for her protesting body to accept the contents of the glass.

The technician asked Julie to lie on her back, propped up on her elbows. Then she directed Julie to the console itself, which was only slightly bigger than the Sony in the Tummyvision commercial. The console was hooked up to a keyboard which the nurse operated. It looked like a typewriter keyboard, but more complex.

"The purpose of the ultrasonogram," Bain started when everything was in place, "is simply to give us a picture of how your baby is developing inside you." He pointed to the console. "With it, we can usually see the important formations of the embryo, the position of the umbilical cord and so forth. If the reception is good enough we should see some of the major organs."

Bain stopped and moved his mouth close to Julie's ear, as though to whisper. "And if you're going to have twins or triplets, we'll know in a minute."

"No thank you," Julie chimed in.

"Sorry, but that's out of both of our hands."

Julie shot a glance at her daughter, but Casey was glued to the small TV screen like a child watching Saturday morning cartoons.

The ultrasonogram was humming and the faint smell of electricity was in the air. Suddenly, Julie felt nervous. At Bain's signal the nurse punched a control on the keyboard and the sound increased. After a few more adjustments, she faced Julie, whose belly had already been bared by the doctor.

The compact instrument held by the nurse was connected to the machine by a wire and had a handle that formed an opening on top of the unit.

"This is the sonic sensor," Bain explained. "Have you ever seen any of those old World War II submarine movies?"

"Yeah, sure, my husband is a sucker for them."

Bain grinned, and the smile seemed to take ten years off him. "Well, when the sub locates an enemy ship with sonar, it's pretty much like this. The sensor sends sound waves of a predetermined length into the abdomen, and when they come up against a formation they can't pass through, they register the impact as a white dot on the screen. Since we're sending a lot of sound waves, they all strike the formation continuously, and we get a lot of white dots, which together form an image."

"And in this case, the formation is the baby," Casey added.

Julie went back to the sonic sensor and thought of the sonic alarm boxes Robert had installed at home, feeling a sudden chill.

Over the next few minutes the nurse pressed the sensor to different parts of her belly, moving it slowly from side to side and up and down. Every now and then she rested it on one spot, moved some dials on the keyboard, and when she was satisfied, she pressed a button, clicking something inside the unit. She was taking pictures, she explained eventually. Then, while Julie kept her eyes trained on the monitor, Bain ordered the nurse to get a close-up shot, and the mass of indistinguishable fuzzy dots moved forward in the picture. Suddenly an unmistakable image became defined.

"That's his head!" Julie exclaimed all at once. "Will you look at that. My baby's head!"

Bain's eyes were on the set, too. "A very good head, I might add. His or hers. Grid," he said to the nurse.

At his command, the nurse punched another key and a calibrated scale appeared on the screen. The nurse moved it around until it matched the field size of the embryo's image, and Bain could take a direct measurement.

"Absolutely normal," he declared a few seconds later.

While he spoke, there was a sudden blurring of the dots, and as soon as the nurse played with another control, the focus cleared and Julie shrieked with surprise.

"He's moving! Look, his head just tilted! And there's his hand!"

Near the center of the screen a small group of white dots grew brighter, then fainter, and repeated the changing pattern again.

"And a strong heart," Bain said with obvious satisfaction.

"Can you tell which it is, yet? I mean a boy or a girl?"

"Tell you now and take all the drama out of it?" Bain quipped. "Why don't we just hold off on that and wait for the results of the amniocentesis?"

Casey looked at the image one last time, then at Julie.

"Well, what do you think, sweetheart?" Julie asked, anxious to finally get a reading from her daughter. "Or is it going to take a TV camera to find out what's going on inside of you?"

Casey's expression became serious. It took a few more seconds, but then she said softly, "I think it's a miracle, not just the picture and all that, but the whole thing, the whole life process. I think I've always kinda taken it for granted, before."

Julie nodded and Casey came closer. "But the main thought I'm thinking is that it's absolutely terrific. I'm really happy for you, Mom. I can't wait. Really!"

Julie beamed at her daughter. "I can't tell you how happy that makes me, Case."

"In fact," Casey added, "I like the idea so much I think I'm gonna have one, too."

Julie raised up quickly and made a playful feint toward her, and Casey backed away.

"Kidding, just kidding," she said with her hands up in surrender.

"Do anything you want," Julie moaned as she got off the table and hobbled toward her, then continued past. "Just don't get between me and the bathroom!"

21
Wilton, Connecticut

AT FIRST GLANCE, SOMEONE FROM THE NEIGHBOR-
hood might have thought the man in the vintage Lincoln had suffered a paralyzing stroke. He hadn't
shown any activity since he'd driven onto the quiet
block and parked by the curb an hour or so earlier. He
just sat staring across the street at the modest two-
family house it had taken him all afternoon to locate.

The brooding residence was itself a paradox. The
house, though obviously not opulent, was on an unusually large parcel of land which set it at a distance
from its neighbors on all four sides. Since the land in
that area was costly, the owners had apparently traded
comfort for privacy. Although he'd never been there
before, the strange visitor knew it was the address of
the person for whom he was looking. What he didn't
know was what he would do if and when he actually
saw him.

It had started only as a theory that aroused his
curiosity, but since then, the three separate reports
he'd seen in the newspapers had formed a disturbing

pattern; before long his theory had turned into a macabre preoccupation. After the first story about the Weston woman and the reported attempt on her life at the railroad crossing, there was a hiatus, but then there had been the horrifying murder of her agent in New York. More recently he'd read about the death threat to her daughter. The papers had followed all the incidents in a continuing story, and in the end he knew if his suspicions were correct what was certain to follow would be even worse. Now the events had finally compelled him to a personal investigation, no matter how physically taxing. The only other way was to reveal the secret, something he'd vowed never to do.

He had come to the narrow street before dark, and now that night was well-established, he waited for a light in the window or a face or any activity that could serve as a clue. But so far there had been nothing. The only traffic was a single car that turned into the block and went by without slowing. He resolved to stay until his strength began to ebb and he could still manage the long ride home to Woodbury. If he found out nothing this time, he would come back. It was only a matter of time, and it was something he absolutely had to do. The awful truth was that he bore responsibility for the murders, the one that had already happened and those to come.

Settling under the cover of darkness, the old man thought back to an earlier time still vivid in his memory. A year after giving up the boy, his own illness had put him in a long coma from which he was not supposed to have awakened. Miraculously, he had. Later had come the blessed remission that astounded the medical teams and himself. Then, perhaps out of self-interest as well as concern, he'd commissioned reports from well-paid private investigators. In the beginning the information had been favorable. The boy enjoyed good health and was stable emotionally, so there was never a need for intervention. Throughout it all, whenever he was conscious, his main interest in life, perhaps his only interest, was the boy.

He'd gotten out of bed after his years of illness to find himself old and lame but with enough mobility for a tolerable life. But by then, the reports were already mixed about the boy's condition, and in the last year they'd become shockingly negative. The boy had begun to suffer long periods of erratic and often antisocial behavior. The first declines were followed by quick rebounds, but over the entire period the intervals had shortened. The pattern was clear. It was the onset of the condition he'd identified in the boy's childhood.

Characteristically, the affliction surfaced some time after the fourth year but, for unknown reasons, went underground thereafter, and usually lay dormant throughout the teens. The old man could never know with certainty whether the Routella had come to his boy randomly or for the *other* reason. The biochemical problem itself was hard to identify and it was surprising he'd been able to diagnose the rare disease correctly in the first place. It took the uncommon perseverance of someone with an intense personal stake.

One of the maddening dilemmas with Routella was that the bizarre behavior patterns it caused often led to its false identification as a psychological sickness.

Without warning, specific brain-wave abnormalities would interrupt or delay the transmission of signals from the cerebral cortex and thus any and all parts of the body, different ones each time, could be affected. It was also why a personality change could erupt at any moment and why results could vary so widely in patients. Once the grip of the sickness tightened, the victim suffered feelings of great rage and violence, alternating with severe depression and loneliness. The symptoms were often accompanied by the belief that one was a misfit.

The symptoms themselves were hellishly frustrating, and it was common for them to alienate those who lived around the sufferer. Some victims acted possessed, with continuous screaming, spitting and burping, even periods of barking like a dog. Half of all the known cases were given to bouts of coprolalia, the involuntary utterance of obscene words. Sometimes there were tormenting tics or twitching that would rapidly migrate from one part of the body to another.

But Routella victims also had a remarkable, if unnerving, talent. Often for long periods of time they could completely suppress all of their symptoms, until there was an inevitable explosion from the damned-up feelings. The long respites gave false hope to the afflicted, who believed themselves cured. But then the new attacks dashed all hope for both the victims and those treating them.

Throughout his childhood, the boy had also shown that he was unaffected intellectually; in fact, he possessed reasoning powers well in advance of his peers.

Then, as now, the drug treatment was effective at

suppressing the symptoms once they occurred, and his early use of it made it even more successful. The fact that early reports on the boy were good was an indication the drug treatment had continued; but now, if his suspicions were correct, either he'd stopped taking the drug or the syndrome had somehow overpowered it.

Of course, that was something he would never know until he'd had a chance to observe him, or, if he dared, to actually speak with him. That was why he was there, why he remained out in the dark night air until well past his normal hour for bed, getting cold, getting old, and waiting.

JUNE
The Sixth Month

22
Milbrook, Connecticut

IT WAS THE BEGINNING OF SUMMER, MORE THAN TWO months since Artie's unsolved murder, nearly half a year since the original scare at the house. Even though there had been no more incidents since the call to Casey, Julie was unable to keep her mind off the danger for very long. It was likely the lack of new developments was only part of the sick, calculated game the madman was playing—although that could not be known for sure. Now all Julie could do was wait for the next move, certain it was only a matter of time—wait and watch her blood pressure slowly rise. So far the diet and medications had not been enough to significantly lower the high readings Bain recorded during the last two visits. Obviously, the game was having another dangerous effect not even the madman could have planned.

At Bain's suggestion Julie saw a therapist for a few visits, in order to help her cope with a number of depressing feelings that might have gone beyond the fear of losing the baby. However, when the woman psychiatrist finally admitted Julie's worries were completely rational and certainly not neurotic, there was little point in continuing.

Meanwhile, there were no new leads on the killing, itself. Artie's funeral was one of the saddest days of Julie's life. The cemetery had overflowed with many friends, famous and not-so-famous, whose lives had been touched by a corny old comic who had only wanted to make people love him. His passing was the end of an era, and only the loss of her father, years before, had left Julie feeling so utterly empty.

Further checking in the local area had uncovered one interesting fact, according to Scotty Mallor. Thomas Gillick, the developmentally-handicapped boy who lived up the block, *had* disappeared from school during part of the day on which Julie had been harassed at home. Gillick had been interviewed by a school psychologist who confirmed that the boy was occasionally disoriented, but showed no signs of being violent. It was doubtful, too, that he had the intellect to coordinate the spider prank, let alone the encounter with the van. On the other hand, there was a certain similarity between the childish scrawl on the note and the natural writing style of the boy. But there was a convenient explanation for this, too. The writing of all the small town's children was similar because most of them had been taught by the same teacher, a strict Palmer-method widow who'd been in the system for over thirty years.

There were no other suspects, and as much as Julie tried to lose her paranoia, it was still difficult for her to walk the streets, to drive, to shop, or perform any of the common activities normal people did, without the same thought. Invariably Julie found herself examining the faces of the men she passed. Often, if they smiled, either out of recognition or simple friendliness, she found herself reading a deeper, more sinister meaning into the gesture. Frequently, she saw herself dispatched from this life in one or more hideous ways until, breathless from fright, she had to force herself back to reality.

There was one tangible proof of her new emotionality; she began to dress more plainly so as not to attract attention. Much of her prettiest maternity clothing—especially the wilder items to which Robert jokingly referred as her post-hippie stuff—stayed in the closet. Perhaps it was a small thing to others, but Julie had always used clothing to mirror her normal buoyant mood.

But the mornings were still fresh, and the afternoons now hot enough to lounge around the freeform stone pool they'd built at the edge of the thick woods. She was accompanied by Rachel Cornell, a pleasant, silent nurse-bodyguard whom Robert had hired the week after Casey had received the threat. And there was time to think about the baby, and about the baby and about the baby. . . .

A loud "kerplunk" interrupted Julie's thoughts as she sunned herself next to the pool. A slender, young pool boy grinned up at her and she was immediately annoyed. His gaze lingered a bit too long, and a bit too low. Her breasts were much larger now, and he had trouble taking his eyes off them. Horny little boy, she thought.

The kid was part of the new parade of people who came to visit Julie once or more a week. It was Robert's idea to populate their home every day in his own absence, a sort of loose ring of protection. Robert now worked shorter hours and returned home by five-thirty.

On any given day, Julie could hope for a visit from close friends who were willing to drive the hour and a half from the city. Also, there were fellow actors and actresses in the area and a few homemakers with whom she'd become friendly. The police still patroled regularly near their home, and checked in daily. It was, perhaps, the most they could do, but with the passage of uneventful time they'd begun to miss days every now and then. Casey was home for the summer now that her sophomore year was over, and Julie took it as an opportunity to make further headway in their relationship. Since the scare at Wellesley the two had been mutually supportive, and the baby had become a frequent and comfortable topic. Casey seemed to welcome a new family member nearly as much as Robert, and had adopted an almost parental concern over the smallest details in Julie's pregnancy program.

Before the present accommodation between them, Julie's acting success had often made Casey resentful of the attention paid her, yet by the time she'd received the accolade in Hollywood, Casey was actually becoming boastfully proud of her. In total, Julie could

sense the start of their long-awaited friendship, and
she welcomed it with open arms and heart.

Naturally, Casey's company was all the more welcome because of the stressful situation at home. When
Robert discouraged a part-time summer job so she
could be around the house more, Julie argued against it
on principle. But she had to admit she was glad when
Casey sided with her husband. She had agreed to
become part of a talent showcase in a nearby rep
theater, and she was busy getting her act down at
home. Julie found it intriguing to think Casey might
end up in show business, although she wasn't sure
how she felt about it. It was also disconcerting to
know she had a daughter old enough to be halfway
through college, and she knew exactly how she felt
about that. Ancient.

Deciding it was a good time to check the mail, Julie
eased off the redwood lounge chair, slipped on a
terrycloth robe and made her way to the road where
the mailbox stood as a marker for the house. Going for
the mail was one of the comfortable rituals that made
her feel at home and countrified.

She reached inside the box and took out a cluster of
envelopes and the new summer L. L. Bean catalogue.
After latching the metal box she stood facing the open
meadow that bordered their home to the south, and let
her eyes take it all in. It was an idyllic setting. Summer
was happening all at once, and the thick, spidery
brambles of only a month earlier were already a profu-
sion of twisting vines and wildflowers. Across the
road, the pure brook water that wended its way from

high in the distant hills was gurgling over mossy rocks. Down the road "a piece," as she loved to say in letters to friends, the brook crossed under the road and continued under overgrown evergreen shrubs on their land until it spilled down into the woods over a quaint stone waterfall.

Nearing the house, Julie studied the simple but charming shape of their nest and thought of the love the original builders must have put into it almost three hundred years before. Living in a home of such age and character, she often thought of the other families that had resided there, loved, suffered, and, perhaps, died there. She'd come to realize that no one ever really owns a home like that; one just uses it for a time, then passes it on to the next owner. It was actually a comforting thought. It was continuity.

When she was back in the house the letter she hadn't seen fell onto the desk from inside the Bean catalogue, and when she saw it, her mind instantly flashed to the nightgown receipt and St. Maarten. She sat down and stared at the empty space on the front where there should have been a return address. Then with hands trembling, she took the letter at arms' length, debating whether or not to wait for Robert's return only a few hours away. A few moments later she drew a deep breath, let it out and opened the letter quickly.

The page contained only a list of a half-dozen names. The first, Artie Shore, had a red crayon line through it. Next came Mickey Lee, then her ex-husband, TJ; then Casey, then Robert. The last name on the list was *Mommy*.

156

23
Wilton, Connecticut

THE ENTIRE ROOM HAD BECOME THE FRONT CAR OF
the Cyclone and when it started going down the big
hill he gripped the sides of his bed for dear life.

Suddenly the killing pains shot up his legs and
exploded like fireballs in his bowels. Lying on his back,
he raced ahead on the runaway Cyclone at blinding
speed. He plummeted precipitously in a steep decline,
only to be suddenly jammed back into the seat as the
Cyclone rose quickly again. He opened his mouth for
an ear-splitting scream but as soon as he got it out, his
throat closed and his stomach tried to empty.

This was the first time the Bitch Goddess was along
for the ride and she fought for the controls in powerful
ways that were new to him. Now it was her cunning
which drove him to the brink of madness and made
him clutch his pillow to his mouth to suffocate his own
cries. The trip was endless and he lay panting, his eyes
open to the flood of crazed pictures pouring into his
mind.

Then, hanging onto the last of his sanity, he could begin to feel the coming of the Savior. Soon, with more authority, the blessed chemical spread its numbing veil of calm over the fury, steadying the Cyclone until finally it slowed and coasted smoothly to a stop at the bottom of the hill.

When the room finally became stationary, he rolled onto one side and willed his eyes closed. In all the years, the Cyclone had never been so terrifying, and he knew this time he'd come perilously close to never getting off.

24
New York City

WHEN HE FOUND THE COFFEE SHOP HE'D SCOUTED
in the theater district, it was overflowing with patrons
and delivery boys, even at the early evening hour.
Now, as he jockeyed for position with the others, he
could feel a strong pulse in his eye and right hand, and
he cursed the familiar afflictions. Gradually he pushed
his way through the crowd until he got to the front of
the line, and when the counterman shot him a glance,
he shouted out his large order.

The order set several dark-haired Hispanic men into
motion. As he waited, someone behind jostled him
roughly; he turned and let out a burst of profanity that
went virtually unnoticed. But it was a mistake and he
knew it. Within a few minutes he left the stifling air
that smelled of perspiration and sticky-sweet buns,
and crossed the street with six coffees on a cardboard
tray. He could see the theater, the well-to-do crowd
milling in front, and the side door he had already
checked.

Just inside the door there was a guard, the first and

only obstacle he would have. Humming tunelessly to himself, he moved toward the door.

When the curtain came down, Mickey Lee knew she had exactly seven minutes to run from the stage to the dressing room, strip down from the scanty Indian maiden's buckskins and get into the brilliant red uniform of a colonial British soldier. Performed for many years, the Independence Day show was a lavish production, especially for the less jaded out-of-town audiences that flocked to Radio City Music Hall for such extravaganzas. It was the grandest of all American history lessons set to music and dance with the Rockettes in full battle dress, portraying both the disciplined British regulars of George III and the suffering, tattered American colonial army.

The show itself boasted one of the most elaborate stage sets of the year with special effects in the final scene, including a fierce snowstorm and dazzling, colorful explosions ignited on and over the stage. More rehearsal time had been spent blocking positions than anything else, and the reason was obvious. As safety-conscious as the technicians might be, if a dancer was in the wrong place at the wrong time, even the limited amount of flash powder used could cause serious injury.

Still breathless from her previous scene, Mickey pulled on her British military hat and prepared for the scene to come. At that moment she felt part of something so much larger than herself, she almost forgot the troublesome thoughts constantly running through her mind, lately, besides the warning about the mad killer just phoned in by Julie: her disappointing career; how lonely and uncomfortable she'd become, living in New York City; whether to return to the small Utah town she'd come from; the people she missed so dearly. Now, onstage at Radio City and in the middle of a spectacular theatrical war, she felt as much a conscripted soldier in her own way as the one she portrayed. She felt empty, displaced in time, a victim of forces beyond her control—unless she took control, which she was about to do.

When the stage manager yelled into the dressing room, a number of Rockettes rose from their seats. Mickey looked down the long line and realized the truth. She was losing herself, as well as her youth. She looked into the mirror and saw the damage that disillusionment had wrought; at that same moment she also knew what she had to do. There were tears of relief forming in her eyes, and, as though experiencing someone else's emotions, she felt her body become energized. This time she'd made an irrevocable decision. Right after the colonists won the war and declared their independence, so would she.

Getting past the guard was insultingly easy. As soon as he entered through the stage door he saw the sentry distracted by a party of older people who had preceded him. He stepped by the guard without waiting, and once out of sight simply turned a corner in the hallway, put the coffee on the floor and made his way to the dressing rooms.

For a moment he thought of waiting for her there. She would be coming by at any moment. Instead, he kept walking past the rooms until he found the door that opened into a darkened area slightly below the stage. Once inside, making sure the door was shut, but unlocked behind him, he let out a sigh of relief. The hard part was over. His plan was working perfectly.

He looked around; his eyes took a few moments to become accustomed to the dimness. He was in the midst of a clutter of musty theatrical paraphernalia. Everywhere there were large klieg lights, old wooden crates, ropes, spools of screening, and dozens of filthy props from productions performed during the history of the theater. Without wasting time, he picked his way silently to the right side of the room, using the sound of the orchestra for guidance. Suddenly he tripped over something with human shape; he froze in fear. Below him was a life-size papier-mâché replica of a cowboy, and when he'd identified it, he had to fight an urge to rip it to pieces. But he had to maintain control, perfect command. He found the small window, took a deep breath, and crept forward, a few inches at a time, toward the light. He could hear the orchestra approaching the finale that would signal the start of the third and final act. Twice before he'd paid money for a good seat close to the stage where he could easily memorize exits, actors and positions—nothing left to chance.

He settled, finally, at the end of the dark room, obscured to both audience and backstage crew. Only a few actors onstage could see him, but they wouldn't be looking in his direction.

As the applause started and the stage curtain separated, he took a seat on a crate he had placed there the

*last time and raised his head into the small opening
that looked out on the stage. Patiently he scanned the
wide stage as it filled with redcoats and colonials. He
searched for the full mouth with one corner that
turned down slightly, the thick light eyebrows, and the
large bosom that would show, even under the starched
uniform.*

*Before the first line of patriotic march music had
begun, he had located Mickey Lee. Cursing her silently, he reached into a deep pocket he'd sewn into
his delivery-boy jacket and felt the cold steel of the .22
caliber Smith & Wesson—with an extended barrel for
accuracy.*

*His handsome, boyish face twisted in hate; he
waited.*

As soon as she'd made her resolution, the show took
on a freshness and novelty Mickey hadn't felt in years.
Confident that the current performance would be her
personal finale, she allowed the richness and color of
the pageant to flow over her, untroubled by any
counter-thought. For once she'd reached an inner
calm and was able to marvel at the dimension of the
living, pulsing festival of which she was a part. After
many years, she again felt the stirrings of pride that
had captured her in the beginning, but that pride, she
knew now, had not truly nourished her spirit. Now she
could recognize it for what it was; an exciting, but
addictive drug.

Onstage, the two forces were mustering for a great
battle, the final conflict that would decide the mock
war. Rockette redcoats kick-stepped into formation on

one side of the broad stage with a precision rivaling any close-order army drill team. Looking down the row of her sister redcoats from the corner of her eye, Mickey saw the simultaneous flashing light of an entire row of knees as they kicked. The brighter the flash, the better their synchronization. Again she felt pride well up at the group's accomplishment. The other dancers had become her family, and it was questionable if she would be able to replace them.

Mickey heard the mournful wail of the oboe, the last moment of relative quiet before all hell broke loose onstage. She could sense the nervousness building among the dancers, and, admittedly, in herself. This was a one-of-a-kind high she was going to miss—*if* she kept to her decision, she found herself thinking.

On command from a redcoat lieutenant, the British troops began marching forward toward the colonials, who began to join ranks. The British formed three close rows of a dozen each, one behind another. As the first file knelt, the other two stood at the ready. When the order was given, the first row would fire in unison while the second row loaded. Then the second row would move forward to become the first row, which would go to the rear of the formation, and the cycle would start over. Thus, a loud volley of shots would ring out every few seconds.

The timpani announced the start of the battle and the first red flares went off onstage, simulating artillery fire. Mickey heard the blood-curdling screams of the colonials when the shells went off around them and saw them rise up to begin their charge. Then she heard the first great volley of shots from her fellow British troops. Suddenly it was as if the guns were real, not just chunks of painted wood. There were two more giant flashes of color on the stage, and another loud burst of gunfire rang out from her own side as snow, dropping from above, began to swirl around all the participants. Smoke began filling the air, too, working its way toward the new front line of British, who raised their guns, heard the rhythmic order and fired, mowing down a large number of the enemy, who fell in mock-agony.

Mickey's row was next, and together with the other eleven in her file, she moved forward a step, dropped to one knee and raised her weapon. She felt exhilarated by the excitement of the performance. Then, suddenly, in the midst of the raging storm and a host of special effects, she spotted something unusual. She'd just turned her head to the left, back to the rear of the stage; for an instant she thought she'd seen a tiny flash of light, a pinpoint of brightness that seemed puny, compared with anything happening around her, but strange, because it didn't belong there.

The slight flash of light from behind the stage, and the single, muffled report of the pistol, went unseen and unheard by the other performers as the battle passed its peak fury and began to subside. By then most of the cast lay as casualties, bloodied and scattered about the stage like broken toy soldiers. The audience had been spared nothing in the way of theatrical gore.

As Mickey began a planned fall, she felt something sharp and fiery take a stitch in her right side. Her first thought when she looked down and saw a red smear forming on her uniform was that they'd used the gelatin-dye bullets, after all. It was an unnecessary effect, she thought.

Suddenly she felt her side fill with fire. She slumped to the stage, facing away from the audience, another dancer near her feet. As the applause rose and the audience came to its feet, Mickey felt the fire travel to the base of her back and race up her spine. Oddly, she found herself wishing she was under the goosedown quilt grandma had made for her in the old house on Dexter Street.

There was a final explosion onstage, a massive cannon barrage that wiped out both sides and made its symbolic message clear. In the distraction of light, sound and pain, Mickey's eyes found the place where the pinpoint of light had appeared. In place of the light was a man, staring out at her.

Before she blacked out she saw a mad smile bloom across the man's young face. Then there was nothing at all.

The stage manager passed within a few feet of him and never noticed the tense youth. The effects crews were still too busy securing equipment to worry about him when another voice screamed a warning from the prop area behind the stage. The door guard responded to the sudden alert and rose from his piano-stool chair, moving squarely into his path. When the guard held up his hand and called for him to stop, he simply increased his pace, and at the last second threw a punch that caught the guard solidly behind the jaw.

The guard crashed back into the wall with a wet smack and fell, unconscious, to the floor.

With no one else between him and the outside door, the boy simply walked outside and was quickly lost in the midst of dozens of Broadway theater parties. Blood surging through him, he moved triumphantly down the street. A moment later he was gone.

25

Milbrook, Connecticut

IT HAD BEEN OVER AN HOUR SINCE THE REPORTER had called with the numbing news about Mickey, and since then, the hopelessness that had swept over her and racked her body with psychic pain began to feed on its own energy. It was a separate, living force that she could not resist.

Nor was the fear new to her. In the recent months it had been a constant, shadowy companion. What was so frightening this time was the speed with which it came on and its astonishing depth.

Images of Mickey flashed crazily in her mind. Mickey lying on the stage, the life flowing out of her. Mickey in pain, not knowing why, already alone in the world, dying without anyone who loved her nearby, or anyone even aware of it.

Then Julie saw herself, also alone, sprawled out on a

floor somewhere unfamiliar. Tears streamed down her face. She felt self-pity and guilt; one fed the other and they became an indistinguishable, taunting horror.

For the first time she understood, felt the immutable truth. The nightmare would continue. It would never end, born out of some unknown hatred, now relentlessly growing stronger and stronger, readying its final assault.

JULY
The Seventh Month

26
Bethel, Connecticut

DETECTIVE MEL PIERCE DROVE AT EXACTLY FIFTY-five miles per hour with one hand on the wheel while the other reached into the crowded inside pocket of his sports jacket. He'd been placed on special assignment from the NYPD after the brutal murder of Artie Shore had been followed by the attempted murder of Mickey Lee.

Pierce pried the two pieces of evidence out of his pocket and laid them on the seat next to him. Before the Lee shooting the knife used on Artie Shore had been the only clue, but even before the lab guys reported an absence of fingerprints he guessed the murder weapon would probably lead nowhere. The knife was the kind that could be purchased in any sporting-goods store in the country, a five-inch, chrome-plated hunting Bowie with a hard rubber handle, more suitable for gutting animals than anything else. The way it had been used on Artie Shore suggested the inexperience of the killer. It had simply been inserted into the victim's back and not twisted the way a trained killer would have done. Only the entry point directly behind the heart and the power with which it was driven accounted for the instantaneous death. It could easily have been a botched job. Artie Shore had been unlucky.

There had been no clue to the age—or even sex—of the murderer until the Radio City guard had given the description of his assailant. According to the guard it was a man of only twenty or so, tall, with straight blond hair and a muscular control problem of some sort. The age made the connection to Julie Weston all the more solid, given the account of the previous attacks, the notes, and the call to her daughter.

But the description wasn't going to be much help, at least not yet. Which left the watch, the only real place to start. Pierce picked up the brown envelope that contained the watch and emptied it into his lap. They'd found it near the fallen guard, its band snapped from the force of the killer's blow. Both the casing and band were solid gold and probably weighed four or five ounces. At current prices, he guessed it would bring upwards of two thousand dollars.

There were fingerprints on the timepiece, but they, too, had led nowhere. After exhausting the criminal print libraries of the three adjacent states, Pierce had also checked the birth records of all area hospitals for fingerprints, especially those from around twenty years ago. But either the suspect had been born elsewhere or somehow the records of his birth had been lost. The search had produced nothing. The prints had also been sent to the FBI in Washington, and there had been no more success there, either. Thus, the watch might have been as useless as the knife, except for the one break. He picked up the watch and read the inscription again: *To Theodore, with unending love, from Father.* The date on it was 1965.

In the years since the inscription, the continuous pressure of skin had worn down the soft metal and the letter definition had been weakened. Unaccountably, the word *father* was a good deal less distinct than the rest, evidently due to the fact that it had been touched more. Pierce squinted at the back of the watch and wondered whether the extra attention to the one word was an effort by the wearer to connect to the father, or obliterate the memory.

The breakthrough had come from the lab, where they'd found at the very edge of the casing three more characters, LHG. The letters turned out to be the signature of the jeweler and not the father, as Pierce had first suspected. It was an identifying mark registered with a jewelers' association headquartered in Boston, but whose membership extended south to New Jersey. The mark was used to identify the craftsman and for insurance purposes in case of theft. The association had been contacted and the jeweler, Lawrence H. Gothe, was identified. Although still on the membership rolls, Gothe was in his upper eighties and in retirement.

Twenty minutes after leaving the highway, Pierce found what he was looking for. The Gothe residence in Bethel was a neat, older home on a modest plot of land near the center of town. The well-tended grounds

173

showed both the time and patience of the caretaker, qualities not inappropriate to a retired jeweler. Later, despite his wife's agitated protests to join them, Gothe quickly maneuvered Pierce outside where they could confer alone. Oddly, as they walked down the steps of the front porch, Pierce noticed Mrs. Gothe's expression had changed from hurt to amusement. She suddenly seemed to be getting a kick out of her husband's belligerent response to her request.

The squat, bald jeweler smelled faintly of Vicks Cough Drops and sat so close to Pierce that their knees almost touched. It was a good ten minutes before Pierce could drive a wedge into Gothe's answer to his first question. The old gent seemed starved for conversation, and his flood of words contained a bizarre mixture of memories, opinions and suspicions, especially some references to his wife in whom he suspected the very mental deterioration which he was so amply demonstrating. But when Pierce produced the gold watch from his pocket and presented it, Gothe fell suddenly silent. His attention to the piece seemed to transport him, and for the first time he looked eager to listen instead of speak.

"Where did you get it?" he asked with complete lucidity.

"We found it in a theater in New York after the commission of a crime. Do you recognize it?"

Gothe stared at it, turning the watch over in his shriveled yet strangely delicate hands until his eyes went to the rim of the casing. At the age of eighty-seven his vision was evidently still acute. For a few moments old movies seemed to be playing in his mind,

174

and when he was again ready to speak, he met Pierce's intense gaze with a nostalgic sigh.

"He was a very good man," he said softly. "Very good but very tragic. I remember."

"The watch is yours?"

Gothe nodded. "Many years ago. I never thought I'd see it again. That's the way it usually is in my work. You make beautiful things, then never see them again."

"What do you remember about it? It's very important."

"What's so important?" the old man asked quickly.

"We believe whoever left the watch behind may be responsible for . . . for committing a number of crimes in New York City. Serious crimes," he added.

"How serious?"

"Murder."

The jeweler briefly registered surprise, then continued to stare at the timepiece. In a few moments his eyes were misty and he seemed to be near tears. When he spoke his voice wavered.

"It was the year after we bought this house." For a second his head turned to the residence, then snapped back to Pierce. "The man was a doctor, well-respected and wealthy. He came to me in sorrow . . . wanted me to create this for his son." He paused again. "It was a good-bye present."

"Good-bye? Who was leaving?"

Gothe pointed to the inscription. "This is what makes me remember, his message, not the watch itself. I've made many watches, but never with such a sad message."

"Why do you say *sad*, Mr. Gothe? It sounds like a fairly standard kind of . . ."

"Not if you knew the way it was meant," Gothe interrupted sharply. He pointed to the second word. "Unending? You see that? I remember the look on his face. The word had a specific meaning for the doctor. You see, he wanted his son to remember him . . . to remember him because his own life was ending." Gothe looked at Pierce and shook his head sadly. "Do you see what I mean?"

"Not exactly, Mr. Gothe. Whatever you can tell . . ."

"I learned about it later. He was asking me to create a legacy, something that would survive him."

Pierce waited as the old man turned the watch over and over in his hands.

"It was some kind of rare disease, an aging sickness as I recall. He was only forty or so but looked much, much older. He told me he didn't have more than a year, and that's the last I ever heard."

"Do you remember his name?"

Gothe ignored the question as though he hadn't heard it. "It was so strange. I never saw him after the first visit. He was so careful with his instructions, yet, when the watch was ready, someone else was sent to pick it up. Perhaps by then he was already too ill."

"It's very important if you can remember his name," Pierce repeated.

Gothe turned toward his home and gestured. "In there. All the files are complete, as always."

"You have the original records on this watch?"

"Everything. From the beginning." Gothe looked at the cop from New York. "I am a jeweler."

"Can you show me those records?"

Gothe nodded and stood wearily, giving the watch back to Pierce. He took a few steps toward the house, where his wife was waiting behind the screen door. As they walked the old man spoke as though a close friend had died.

"Tell me, please. Has the world become such an unhappy place? Can something that once stood for so much love between a parent and his child—can it now be a clue to such a terrible crime as you said?"

"I don't think the world is any better or worse than it's always been," Pierce offered softly, not knowing whether he believed the words or not.

Fifteen minutes later, when Pierce was back on the road heading to his motel, he found himself thinking about the sorrow in the old jeweler's eyes. He also thought about the doctor who had had the watch made and who probably had been dead for many years. And he thought about the son, the recipient of the love offering, and wondered what kind of boy he must have been, and what he must have become to now be the prime suspect in a terrible murder.

Pierce stared blankly at the scenic Connecticut countryside blurring past him. On a small piece of paper in his chest pocket was the name and address of John Kreuger, the deceased doctor and father who had tried to be remembered and had succeeded in a way he never could have anticipated.

27
Milbrook, Connecticut

"SHE'S RESTING COMFORTABLY," BENJAMIN BAIN said to Robert as he closed the door to Julie's bedroom behind him.

"How dangerous is this kind of anxiety attack?" Robert asked immediately. "And what if it happens again?"

"Emotional panic, even a strong one like she had, isn't itself that dangerous, at least not considering your wife's age. Thirty-nine isn't old and the body is still plenty resilient enough to bounce back."

"Julie's forty, not thirty-nine."

Bain stared at him for a moment and a small smile reached his lips. "I see."

"Is there anything you suggest? Anything we can do?"

"Has anything changed in respect to your . . . situation?"

Robert shook his head. He felt helpless and terribly frustrated.

"Then all I can offer is the same advice: have her

stick to the diet, avoid stress, stay in bed as much as possible." Bain took off his glasses and rubbed distractedly at the deep ridge on the bridge of his nose. "The maternal instinct is intensified during pregnancy. I mention this to point out why this is the most dangerous time. See, the fear that gets Julie into one of these attacks is compounded by the fear of something happening to her baby. Psychology isn't my specialty, but I do know that during an anxiety attack, certainly after a few hours of one, most people reach a point of anger at being frightened, especially after they see nothing has really happened to them except the fear itself. And then they'll try to sort of challenge the fear. It's called proactive inhibition, and what it means is you finally accept the fear and give in to it to see where it will lead."

Robert tried to follow Bain but did not understand where he was headed.

"The point is, when a person gives in, he or she begins to regain control. It's like they've given permission to the fear and therefore can become superior to it. But in Julie's case, she can't do that because even though she can risk herself, she won't risk the baby."

"So she never gives in?"

"That's right. She continues to fight it, and thus continues to be controlled by it."

"It's a beautiful little catch-22 situation, isn't it?" Robert said. "Jesus."

"We've got hospitalization as an alternative, should it be necessary. My feeling is to try and avoid that if possible. Familiar surroundings are generally better."

"Okay," Robert said wearily. He led Bain to the

door where the doctor turned and gripped his hand.

"Remember, I'm always available. Don't hesitate."

Robert looked up at the kindly face. "Thanks. It means a lot."

"And you try to take it as easy as possible, too."

As Bain walked down the driveway to his car Robert thought, How? How in God's name do I do that?

Julie awoke in bed, not knowing how she'd gotten there from the floor. She'd been alone when she fainted. There was a purple welt on her right elbow and a bump on her scalp. She vaguely remembered falling, remembered the way the room had darkened around the edges of her vision, and then suddenly had narrowed completely.

With difficulty she stood and walked to the window. Her legs were rubbery, and there was a slight gauze between her eyes and the world, the way it felt when she ran a high temperature. The sedatives were still working, maybe keeping her sane.

Then there was a gentle tapping at the door and Casey entered her room. The look in Casey's eyes also telegraphed fright and brought her own emotions instantly to the surface again. Moments later she found herself in her daughter's arms, feeling the tears rolling slowly down her cheeks.

28

Danbury, Connecticut

AN ANNOYED KAREN DAVENPORT PUSHED THE phone's hold-button and buzzed her boss on the intercom. When Robert Montgomery picked up, she told him the caller had refused to give his full name but claimed to be a close friend of the family. "All he'll say, Mr. Montgomery, is that it's TJ."

Surprised, Robert paused momentarily, then quickly said, "Put it through."

"I realize this is awkward," TJ began after introducing himself, "but under the circumstances I felt it was better to talk to you than to Julie."

"I appreciate that," Robert answered, uneasiness rising in him.

"Something's happened here in L.A. I think you should know about. I'm aware of what's been going on with Julie because Casey has kept me filled in."

"What's happened?" Robert braced, sitting up in his chair.

TJ hesitated. "Could you tell me first if anything has . . . I mean is Julie all right?"

"She's okay. Dealing with this latest thing is very hard."

"What do you mean?"

"A few days ago another one of Julie's friends was hurt. The police assume it's the same man who's been threatening us."

"Who?"

"Mickey Lee." Robert was about to add something when he heard TJ's sharp intake of breath. Since they'd been friends for so long, Robert realized, TJ must know Mickey very well.

"She's going to be okay. She was shot onstage, was critical for a day, and now is in satisfactory condition."

"Thank God for that." And again there was another pause.

"TJ, can you tell me why you've called? I assume it concerns Julie."

"I think it does. This morning I got a piece of mail addressed to me. It looked harmless enough, but something about it made me stop before opening it."

"You got a threat? Another one?"

"Worse. A letter bomb is what the police called it. I don't think it was meant to kill me because there was a note in it and I guess the creep wanted me to read it, which I couldn't have done if the whole thing had blown up. Any idiot could have made the device, according to the cops. Just some flash powder and stick matches rigged to a string. You open the letter from the top and the string pulls the matches along sandpaper. Anyway, it didn't even go off, but whoever sent it scared the hell out of me."

"What did the note say?"

"That's the craziest part. It said, 'You never should have let Mommy do it.' Mommy was all in capitals and the thing was written in a kid's printing style, like a second- or third-grader, even done on cheap brown paper."

Robert sat back in his chair, pressing a hand over his eyes. The news was just one more piece of evidence that the killer knew a lot about Julie's life, and not just from the movies. And that he'd again demonstrated he could get to anyone, even someone who knew he might be coming.

"It's not the first time he's used that term to address Julie," Robert said. "He's called her that from the beginning, when we thought it was only a prank. Obviously we're dealing with someone who's not only crazy, but who for some reason has connected himself to Julie. And now he's torturing her."

A few seconds elapsed before TJ spoke, and now there was vulnerability as well as indignation in his voice.

"Well, there's a whole new twist on this 'Mommy' business, I'm afraid." Robert heard TJ take a breath, as if steeling himself. "I don't know what this means any more than you will," he went on, "but at the top of the note, where the creep addressed it to me, well, instead of using my name it just says 'to Daddy.' "

AUGUST
The Eighth Month

29
Milbrook, Connecticut

IF ANYONE HAD BEEN ABLE TO SEE THE LOOK WITH
which Casey raised the garage door, or how she
stroked the low roof, or the way she entered the front
compartment, as though it were a spiritual inner sanc-
tum, he would have realized that, for Casey, the 1970
green Mercedes 280SL convertible was true love.

In addition to being elegant transportation the
Mercedes, and the music that played inside, became a
sanctuary where she could be alone. It was a place she
could break the rules and get away with it. More than
once she'd been pulled off the road by village police in
Milbrook and Wellesley, radio blaring, only to charm
her way into a reprimand, rather than a ticket. The car
was also a concrete token of the love her mother felt
for her.

The quiet inside the car heightened Casey's alert-
ness to possible danger. It was dark and she'd had to
sneak past Rachel to get out, but the urge to bolt the
guarded house had been overpowering. Her hand
found both front door locks within seconds of her

entry; then she leaned back and inhaled the familiar scent of old leather. She started the car and rolled it backwards into the driveway without lights. A few moments later she was doing close to sixty on the narrow, winding country road that led north to Bridgewater.

Casey exhaled deeply and waited for the familiar sense of relief that usually accompanied being alone in her car, but this time the sense of dread she'd felt in the darkness on the way to the garage did not abate with distance. There was something wrong, and a sixth sense told her whatever it was would stay with her no matter how far she traveled. In a flash of panic she realized she'd forgotten to look behind her to the rear compartment. Before she became too afraid to do it, she drew a breath and jerked her head around, ready to scream.

No one was there. She *was* alone. Still shaking, she turned her attention to the road. There were no streetlights. The shadowy shapes outside were menacing, each of them a potential ambush. Her lower lip throbbed and she realized she must have bitten into it, from fright. She pushed a button on the Blaupunkt, and rock music pumped into the car's small inner space.

The idea of making a U-turn at the junction of 67 and heading back to the safety of home occurred to her even before she began to tire of the pounding music. For some reason the escape had not brought the expected relief, and the feeling she was being stalked was actually increasing. Thinking of her mother's anxiety episode, she began to hyperventilate and cracked open a window. Casey opened the glove compartment and rummaged through a stack of loose cassettes, her eyes still on the road. She could see reflecting in her lights the sign for 67, about a quarter of a mile ahead.

The sign was only a few seconds away when she remembered the cassette she wanted was already in position in the tape deck. Her hand played over the dark surface of the stereo facade, came to a loose, flat edge and shoved it back until it clicked into place. She heard the sound heads closing over the thin band of tape and the sprockets turning. Casey waited impatiently for the hissing of tape leader to dissolve into the strong, husky lament of Jesse Foxboro. When it stopped, there was another sound, a voice, but younger than Jesse's, the weird, high-pitched voice she had heard once before on a telephone in her dorm.

"Casey and Mommy and Daddy make three." It said it over and over. It sang it.

Then the voice ended and the obscene, mocking laughter began.

When Casey burst into the house, her mother and Robert were in the living room with two Milbrook policemen, whose cars she'd spotted in the drive, and Rachel, her mother's bodyguard. Before she could blurt out a word about the cassette, her mother breathlessly said, "They've just caught him out in the woods."

"What?" Casey fairly shouted.

"It turns out we know him, too."

"Who is it?"

"Billy, the kid from down the block who used to

take care of the pool. The one Robert fired, remember?"

Casey's mouth dropped open in disbelief. "Billy Drayton? You don't think he could be . . ."

"We don't know for sure," Robert interjected, "but he matches the description of the Radio City guy. Tall, blond and young."

Casey had spoken with Billy on more than a few occasions, and her impression was that he was definitely weird, fairly immature, and darn good-looking.

"How did they catch him?"

"Rachel was walking the grounds on her nightly routine and she heard something moving in the woods. At first, she thought it was a deer and that it ran off when she got close, but she kept going and managed to sneak up on Billy, hiding in the bushes. He had binoculars with him." Julie paused, unconsciously pulling her robe more tightly around her. "She says she thinks he was trying to look into our bedroom window while I was changing into my nightgown.

"They found some pictures that Billy had with him and tried to ditch, one in particular that makes my skin crawl." Julie drew a deep breath and continued. "It's a shot of me that he took at the pool when I wasn't looking. The picture isn't very clear but clear enough to see I'm not wearing anything on top. I was sunbathing half in the nude when he snapped it. And there was another one, harder to make out. He must have tried to get it right through the bedroom window at night. You can just make out the shape of a man and woman in bed. Guess who?" She laughed bitterly. "And I won't tell you what we're doing."

"Christ," Casey said, disgusted. Then she saw there was something else bothering her mother. "What aren't you telling me?"

Julie rubbed at her forehead and Casey could see her fingers trembling.

"The damn nude picture had writing on it. The little bastard drew circles around my breasts and . . ." For a moment Julie almost lost it, but held on to her emotions. "And another around where the baby is."

Casey felt a cold hand touching her body all over. She shivered in disgust.

"What does it mean?"

"I don't know," Julie said.

"Mom, there's something else," Casey said, launching into a brief description of the cassette incident.

When Casey had finished, Julie sighed deeply. "Well, we won't have to worry anymore, will we?" She stared at the pathetic boy in the next room, slumped in a chair, head down, and suddenly had the oddest thought: *It's not him. It won't stop. Not now. Not ever.*

They spent the next few hours waiting, knowing the search of Billy Drayton's house was as crucial as his capture. Hopefully, it would produce evidence of his larger involvement in Julie's nightmare.

During the time in which Scotty Mallor obtained a warrant, searched the youth's room and returned to the Montgomery residence, Mel Pierce received the news and drove to the house from his nearby motel. His standing request to be notified if anything happened had been honored by Mallor, but it was not without some feeling of exclusion that he patiently waited with the family for further news.

When Mallor finally returned, Pierce took charge in a tacit understanding between the two.

"Short and sweet," Mallor said. "And I think we nailed him." Mallor opened a large envelope and fished out a child's notebook. "Exhibit A, as it were. One lined composition book with several pages missing. And B," he continued, "a sample of the kid's handwriting. It's script, not printing, but I think the paper and colors will match."

Pierce asked for both of the original threatening notes, the first that had come with the spiders, and the one written on the back of the nightgown receipt. They were both in a safe at Milbrook headquarters, although that information did not seem to disconcert him at all.

"Isn't this the standard-issue notebook for all school kids around here?" he asked Mallor. "In other words, wouldn't we be likely to find these items in any number of homes?"

"Obviously," Mallor answered with slight annoyance. "And the writing implements, as well. We checked that out a long time ago. Most of the kids around here are taught by the same teacher, a strict older lady with precise ideas of how each letter should be formed. So even if we got a sample of his earlier writing and it matched, we still wouldn't have any conclusive proof."

Pierce nodded. "On the other hand, we do have a seventeen-year-old kid with a composition book they hand out in second or third grade. Does he have any younger brothers or sisters?"

"Only child," Mallor answered.

"Were his parents home?" Pierce asked.

"Yeah, and they weren't too happy."

"What did they have to say?"

"Well, they were shocked, of course. I've known these people all my life and they just about threw me out of the house. They couldn't believe I was serious. Then, when I showed them the search warrant, they began shouting hysterical stuff about what a good boy their Billy was. It was rough, you know?"

"Did you tell them about the pictures?" Robert growled harshly. "Did you tell them where we found him and what he was doing?"

"Take it easy, Mr. Montgomery," Pierce said evenly.

"Mel, I found pictures," Mallor said. "Three snapshots." He held them out.

"Jesus," Julie cried. "I thought I'd lost them. They're from a family album."

Pierce looked at Mallor. "Damaging," he said simply.

"Yeah," Mallor answered. "And I've been saving the best for last. I don't think anyone is gonna call this circumstantial." He placed a single, wrinkled sheet of paper on the table. "I found this in the boy's wastepaper basket."

Julie looked at the paper, heeding Pierce's warning not to touch it. She saw the now-familiar swatch of red crayon and two words: *dear Mommy*. "That's it," she murmured, and then, suddenly, the tears started. Robert came to her, encircling her shaking figure, and let her cry it out.

"Did you show the note to his parents?" Pierce asked.

"Yeah, I did. They couldn't explain it. Said it didn't even look like his handwriting as a boy, let alone now. Oh, one more thing. Mrs. Drayton isn't the first Mrs. Drayton. It isn't something that's common knowledge around here, but Billy's original mother died when he was young and his father remarried."

"So you're thinking we've got a direct connection here to the use of the 'mommy' thing," Pierce said.

"It's certainly plausible. Maybe all these years the kid's been a little psycho over losing his real mother, and maybe in some way he's still looking for her, say, to get even. It could all tie into the 'mommy' references in the notes."

"It's plausible," Pierce said, without evident enthusiasm, noting the hint of disappointment that flickered in Mallor's eyes. Doubts were working in Pierce, undefined yet familiar enough from years of police work not to be ignored. It was all so neat, so perfect, so coincidental. Pierce didn't like coincidences.

"Well," he said finally, "take the kid in. Start questioning him. What's the situation about keeping a minor under lock and key in Connecticut?"

Mallor's eyes narrowed as he stared back at Pierce. He knew his ego was involved in a way that was not entirely professional, knew that in his own mind, at least, there was a clear competition going on between Pierce and him. He also respected Pierce; the guy was obviously a good cop. "The law is pretty fuzzy on minors—lenient is the word. I doubt they'll let us keep him for very long. The Draytons were on the phone to a lawyer before I'd left the house."

"Get as much as you can," Pierce said. "I've got another idea."

"Something wrong, Detective?" Mallor asked, knowing full well that there was.

"Yeah, Scotty, maybe. I don't know." He shook his head in frustration.

Robert and Julie, holding hands, watched the exchange between the two cops with growing anxiety. Minutes before, they'd had reason to believe their nightmare might be over. But now, suddenly, nothing at all seemed certain. It was almost worse to be in this new, seemingly inexplicable limbo.

"I'll call," Pierce said, and was gone.

30
Ridgefield, Connecticut

PIERCE COULD SMELL THE MONEY AFTER DRIVING twenty minutes south on old route 7 from Danbury. In that time, he'd traveled from an economically struggling old city to the exclusive town of Ridgefield, where the homes were dramatically more affluent.

The address in Gothe's records turned out to be a large, forbidding Georgian residence presently divided into a lawyer's office on the main floor and private living quarters above. The middle-aged professional couple on the second story knew little about the man who had once owned the huge home, only what they'd been told in passing by elder townspeople. They'd heard he'd kept pretty much to himself. They also told Pierce that the house's current owner, Dr. Horace Bethune, lived in the small cottage at the rear of the property, the original guest, or servant's, quarters.

Bethune, a towering, sixtyish man with a rock-hard shell, greeted Pierce at the door to the cottage. Yes, he'd bought the house from Dr. John Kreuger, and after his own wife had died, he'd rented out the larger house and had moved into the cottage. Pierce asked if there was anything he could tell him about the former owner, and in particular, his son. As Pierce questioned the physician his own gaze was deliberately confronting, and bit by bit, the man loosened up. Doctors, like cops, were trained to play their cards close to the vest; in his years on the force, he'd had more than one unpleasant and frustrating experience with the medical profession.

"You may find this curious—I did—but I only actually saw Dr. Kreuger once, at a charity affair. He was pointed out to me but we never spoke."

"Weren't you both surgeons at about the same time?"

"In two different specialities and two different states. My area was ophthalmology, his gynecology."

"When you bought the house, you didn't meet him?"

"It was by proxy. Dr. Kreuger was not present when the house was shown, nor at the closing, itself.

As a matter of fact the building was completely vacant by the time it was shown, which, as I'm sure you know, is not recommended by real estate agents."

"Furnished usually brings a higher price you mean?"

"Exactly. And in all the meetings, Dr. Kreuger was represented by his lawyer, who I understand was subsequently killed in New York in a traffic accident."

"Then there's nothing you can tell me about Kreuger's son, either?"

"Didn't even know there was a child, or a wife, for that matter. You should understand that these were the most unusual of circumstances. In fact, even the neighbors didn't know much about him. Evidently he was a very private man, almost a recluse, except for his practice. Possibly it was because of his status."

"Because of his wealth?" Pierce asked, not understanding the doctor's meaning.

"No, not his wealth. Because he was so widely acclaimed in the field of gynecological research. With all the notoriety he must have had, he probably attracted the . . . let's say, the frantic fringe of patients, women with serious medical problems who had nowhere else to turn. This is not uncommon in any gynecological practice."

At first Pierce didn't follow the implications of Bethune's comments; then, suddenly, he thought he understood.

"We're talking about the period before the legalization of abortion, aren't we?"

Bethune nodded sharply. "I think we understand each other."

"And Kreuger did have a regular practice, as well as his research."

"I think that was the case," Bethune said.

"The one time you saw him, when was that—what year, I mean?"

The doctor thought for a moment. "The middle sixties, I'd say, give or take a few years."

"How did he appear to you? Was there anything unusual about him?"

"As a matter of fact there was. I remember thinking how much the work had taken out of him, the price he'd paid physically."

"Can you be more specific?"

"The poor devil looked like he was falling apart, and I mean that quite literally." Bethune's formal manner began to loosen.

"I'd heard," Pierce said, "that he had some kind of aging disease."

"I wouldn't know about that, of course, but the way he looked, it wouldn't surprise me." Bethune got up from the easy chair and walked across to his living room window to look out at the main house. "I should have thought of this sooner, but it's been such a long time. We did find something of his."

"What?"

"It was about a month or two after we moved into the house." He gestured to the house and there was suddenly a lament in his voice. "When we lived there . . . every trace of the previous occupants had been removed, so much so that my wife and I thought it more than a little odd. Every drawer had been thoroughly emptied, every closet swept and in some cases, rooms had actually been scrubbed."

"Strange."

"Yes, that's what made it so hard to understand what we found in the basement. There was a single, tall file cabinet that had been sealed and put into a crate and nailed shut. We found it quite by accident in a secret closet under the stairs. Obviously the movers had missed it. We opened it to see what was inside; just some of the medical histories of his past patients, as it turned out."

"What happened to the file?" Pierce said, holding back the sudden burst of adrenaline he felt.

"Well, that was the strange part. We tried to reach Dr. Kreuger to return it, but even though it was soon after the move, we couldn't locate him, and his lawyer didn't return our calls. It was as though all traces of him had simply vanished. After I gave up on getting to Kreuger, I contacted a local medical society and later received a call from a research organization I'd never heard of. A few days later a truck arrived and took the file away. That was the last I ever heard of it."

"Can you remember the name of the research organization?"

Bethune's perpetual scowl mellowed for the first time. "As a matter of fact, I can, only because it happened to be the same as a singer my wife and I liked very much at the time. Desmond . . . Johnny Desmond. It was the Desmond Clinic, though I have no idea if it's still in existence. That was a long time ago, fifteen years."

Pierce was satisfied, in fact pleased. He had something concrete going, something that *felt* solid. He thanked Bethune and rose to leave, extending his hand.

"I used to like Johnny Desmond, too," he said. "They don't write them like that anymore, do they?"

Bethune shook the proffered hand, then moved slowly to the door with a hint of stiffness somewhere. "They don't do a lot of things like they used to."

31
Milbrook, Connecticut

FROM HIS HIDING PLACE ON THE HIGH MEADOW, THE murderer could see more of the surrounding area than from any other point nearby. He did not need binoculars to observe the house directly across from him— only the people in it, whenever they came near a window. No one could see him in the tall grass, he was sure—not the police sons-of-bitches protecting her house from the crazy boy, not the unlucky family a few blocks away everyone was blaming for producing the crazy bastard, not the bodyguard and not even the murderous Bitch Goddess, herself, whom he hadn't seen in all the time he'd been spying. There was triumph in the laughter that no one could hear, and the sound so delighted him he let it come again.

His mood had brightened once he had resolved what to do about the old man. It had taken him a long time to figure out who he was, and for a time after the discovery it had made him think he was crazy. The idea had actually occurred to him the first time he'd seen the human skeleton lurking outside his house, when he'd slowly drawn back the bedroom curtains and seen the dark car parked across the street. But who he was and why he was there had required the reading of the Letter.

At first the truth had been too frightening to believe. The period that had followed was an agonizing, confused time and his indecision had kept him awake at night in a pool of sweat. It would have been easier if there had been only the man's deception to deal with, but it had been complicated by another feeling that hadn't gone away. More than once, he had come close to breaking out of the anger. He had wanted to go to the feeble old man, to be held by him and return to the more secure past. But all the spying had made it obvious that the man was, in reality, another enemy. The decision had come quickly after that: the next time they met he would have to punish him like the others, like the miserable runt, Artie Shore, the cheap slut, Mickey Lee.

Incredibly, he felt a twinge of compassion for the idiot kid who had accidentally helped him in his plan. It was strange because many months had passed since he'd cared about anything except revenge. The kid looked a little like him and was close to his own age, and he must have been getting back at the Bitch in his own way. He'd come upon him by accident that night in the woods, while trying to find a safe route to the house. He was remarkably adept at seeing in the dark and cushioning the sound of his movements, and as he'd crept forward, he'd suddenly noticed the light. It had come from inside a thicket of vines in the heart of the woods. At first, he hadn't been certain what or who it was. The growth had been extremely dense, and as he'd approached, he'd momentarily lost sight of the light. Once within several feet of the thicket, he'd crouched without a sound, then leaned in for a closer look. On the other side of the vines there had been a clearing about six feet around, at the bottom, a pressed-down carpet of leaves, and in the center, holding a flashlight, had been the kid.

It had taken just a moment to understand what the thin blond kid was doing, and when it had hit him he'd felt too embarrassed to watch. The kid had been using the flashlight to examine photographs, and it'd been an easy guess that the pictures were dirty. The boy's pants had been down to his knees, and the hand that wasn't holding the flashlight had been working up and down.

Later, at a distance, he'd come up with the idea that seemed too good to be true, and since then everything had happened the way he'd planned. The kid had come to the spot again two nights later, but this time he'd been waiting. This time, he'd followed him back out of the woods and down the road to the kid's house. Then, on an afternoon when the house was empty, he'd broken into the unlocked home and made his way to the upstairs room, the kid's room. Then he'd taken the pictures he'd stolen from Her album months ago, and had dropped them into the back of the desk drawer. He'd left the composition book and crayon under a pile of magazines on the bureau. And he'd crumpled up the piece of paper on which he'd started to write "dear Mommy" and had thrown it into the waste basket. He was particularly proud of that last idea.

His lips curled into a grotesque smile as he raised the binoculars and worked his way along the side of the house, hoping for a glimpse of her, praying for any opportunity caused by an indiscretion or lapse of security. Getting through the net of protection thrown over the house meant risk. The bodyguard was a problem. She watched over Her as though their flesh were joined. There were also more people around than before, drones paying homage to the Queen Bee. Any risk now was unacceptable and unnecessary. Sooner or later they'd become sloppy, all of them. It had happened once before during the long interval between his attacks, and now, if justice was with him, he'd be able to get to her and the baby at the same time.

The binoculars continued to move left, past the den and dining room windows, past the patio to the end of the house. Then they traveled up to the attic, where a limb of the largest sugar maple brushed a tiny window, and he could feel a sudden surge of blood.

Somewhere, the Cyclone was beginning to crank up the big hill and he broke out into a dank sweat. From reflex, he reached into his jacket pocket for the pills, but when he held them in the palm of his hand he looked at them as though for the first time. A few seconds later the clanking became louder in his mind, and his fingers closed in a vise-like grip over the plastic bottle.

The sweat poured out of him as the clanking became one cacophonous roar, pounding relentlessly in his mind. His time, he knew, was coming. Triumph. Glory. Revenge. The pain, he now realized, was his ally. His only friend. The pain was his conscience, directing him to what he must do.

The clanking screamed louder and through his tears he smiled. The time was near.

32
New York City

DURING THE FEW MINUTES IN WHICH THEY WATCHED the lineup, not a single word passed between the observers. Seated in the auditorium, Robert was surprised to find himself thinking of the Draytons, sitting huddled in a small waiting room outside. Within moments, the simple gesture of a man pointing would condemn their son to prison for the rest of his life.

When the room went dark, Robert felt a chill on the back of his neck and waited for the six-man line to form on the stage. Pierce was seated next to him, and the stage door guard from Radio City was somewhere behind them. Pierce was staring straight ahead, deep in thought.

He'd driven them both into the city from Connecticut, and during the trip, Robert had found himself liking the tough detective more and more as they'd talked. But Pierce hadn't shown any eagerness to discuss the interrogation of the Drayton boy. It finally had taken Robert's direct probe to break the ice. And then, he'd learned Pierce was reluctant because he had no place to go with what he'd learned.

"As I expected, the boy never kept any records of his jobs, so he couldn't verify where he was during any of the crimes," Pierce volunteered, "but I *was* impressed by the way he reacted. Most of the guilty ones make up elaborate stories that eventually foul them up, and Drayton never even tried. The whole thing seemed beyond him, like he'd given up or something. Also, he made a few mistakes about how to get to New York. Of course, he could have been deliberately flubbing, but I thought he just wasn't sure of the directions."

"What about the watch? I assume he said it wasn't his?"

Pierce nodded.

"Did you believe him about that, too?"

"Yeah. I thought he was telling the truth. As a matter of fact I'd brought the watch with me and asked him to put it on. First of all, it didn't fit him. Much too tight, although the band is adjustable and could have been changed. But more importantly, he put it on his right wrist when I handed it to him, not what a right-handed person would normally do."

"How do you know the killer is right-handed?"

"The Radio City guard was punched on the right side of his face, and said he was looking directly at his assailant when he was struck. I have to assume at a time like that the attacker would instinctively throw his best punch, using his dominant hand, and it's impossible to hit someone flush on the right side of his face with your left hand if he's looking at you. Therefore, whoever hit the guard was a righty."

Robert glanced over at George Berry, the guard, who seemed relatively at ease. It made Robert wonder whether the procedure held a sense of theater for the slender, bearded man. Possibly he was pleased over the opportunity to gain revenge.

As they waited, Pierce added a last piece of contradictory information about Drayton. Pierce had questioned many of the boy's friends and teachers. What he'd found both added to and detracted from the case. Significantly, the boy had had a "troubled past." He'd been pushed by the school to see a psychiatrist after an incident involving an older female student. However, the doctor's records had shown no concern that the behavior was clinically abnormal and the shrink had gone so far as to say that the "likelihood of violence in Billy Drayton was small." All in all, it had cast further doubt on the youth's guilt.

Without announcement, the spotlights went on with a loud hum from above the stage, startling those waiting below. Then, a precinct sergeant walked to the center of the floor and made a short speech about what was going to happen, addressing his comments without emotion toward the small audience. Finally, he focused on the eyewitness guard whom he instructed routinely. A few moments later, he called to someone unseen to his left, and the first of six young men plodded onto the stage.

One behind another, the line moved uncomfortably forward until the first man was near the wall and was forced to stop in place. The fourth to walk out into the lights was Billy Drayton, and when Robert saw him he had the urge to look away, but then realized the youth couldn't see him through the one-way glass. There was no doubt from his behavior, however, that he was scared witless, and for an instant he stopped walking and looked as if he was going to jump off the stage and run. The kid also looked as if he was about to get sick.

The next thing Robert noticed, when all were in position facing the audience, was the similarity among them. Somehow, he'd thought they'd be more diverse in appearance. But for some reason the attempt here was to confuse the guard, or at least put his powers of recall to an extreme test.

The age range among the six probably varied no more than three or four years. All but one had blond or light-brown hair; Billy's was the blondest. Four of the six were slightly built, and over five-foot-nine on the height lines that ran from wall to wall behind them. Robert looked back at the guard, who sat several rows away, and in the reflected light from the stage he could see the man's eyes moving from one face to another. Then Robert felt a gentle pressure on his arm and turned to meet Pierce's disapproving gaze.

"Uh, uh, don't look back. We don't want to do anything that might interfere," he whispered.

207

"Why do they look so much alike?" he asked quietly.

"Anything less and the I.D. would be liable to be thrown out of court. Don't worry," Pierce added quickly, "if the kid's the one, the guard has a good shot at identifying him."

"If he does, will it convince you?"

"It wouldn't hurt."

One by one, the sergeant asked the youths to step forward and state their names, ages, and occupations. He then asked them to face right, left, and to the back of the stage. The last part of the brief interview was a simple wardrobe change. He asked them to put on a jacket, the same jacket for each of them, and to repeat the turns.

"The coat was described to us by the guard," Pierce said softly. "It might help jog his memory."

The next time he spoke, his voice was barely audible. "By the way, the one on the extreme left is my nephew, and the fifth one is an actor we got from Central Casting."

Robert looked again at the youths, and once he knew who wasn't a criminal it seemed obvious that they were "acting."

After the interviews were over the sergeant commanded them to remain in position, and he left the stage to sit next to the witness. Robert tried to eavesdrop on the exchange but it was too muffled to understand. Then the cop yelled to the stage, asking number two to step forward and put on the jacket again. He repeated the instruction to number six, and then, making Robert tingle with anticipation, he asked the same of number four. There was another long silence after they were back in line, and finally the sergeant stood and stiffly ordered them off the stage.

Pierce shook his head at Robert discouragingly, and moved off toward the sergeant. Ten long minutes later he was back.

"What is it? Something go wrong? Didn't he make the identification?" Robert searched Pierce's face for clues.

The detective sighed long and loud. "Yeah, he came up with an I.D. A very strong one."

Robert waited, impatient that Pierce was dragging the news out.

"He made a positive identification on Bernard Griswold," and again the sigh came, "my goddamn nephew."

SEPTEMBER
The Ninth Month

33

Milbrook, Connecticut

JULIE LAY IN BED WAITING FUTILELY FOR SLEEP. SHE hadn't slept for longer than a few hours in weeks and doubted, now, whether that would change. There were only a few days left, certainly no more than a week, before she would deliver.

Her blood pressure was already close to the number beyond which Bain was going to put her in the hospital. Her house was filled with policemen and a bodyguard. An incessant stream of reporters trying to cover her story were being turned away.

Even the baby seemed to be fighting her now. Her belly had swollen so much in the last week she felt like a ripe melon about to split open. And there was the kicking, the interminable agitated movement that had virtually become a second heartbeat and, for the first time, really hurt. It was something she hadn't expected, and it was confusing to be annoyed with the cherished newcomer.

Enough, she admonished herself. It was time for another accounting. It had worked before, to a degree.

One, she counted resolutely, she was eight months and two weeks into her term and so far she and her baby had escaped the worst of the blood pressure problem. Two, although she missed her daughter more than ever, Casey had come through it safely and was back at Wellesley where she belonged and where, Mel Pierce had assured her, she was safest. Three, Robert was healthy, and dealing well enough with a continuing, unknown menace. Four, she'd kept her weight gain for the entire second half of her pregnancy to under ten pounds. Even Bain had been proud. Five, Mickey was completely out of danger and would soon be released from the hospital. Six, other than the letter bomb, TJ was evidently not a serious target, and her mother had never been touched by the nightmare, except by knowing about it in the first place. Seven, and most important, she was only days away from actually holding her baby in her arms.

Julie lay there waiting for the self-administered dose of logic to calm her quivering. A long time later, when the bed was soaked with perspiration, she added another entry to the ledger. Eight, *there's a maniac out there, a monster who wants to destroy me.*

Julie stared up at the ceiling, feeling Robert sleeping at her side, and tried to blink back her tears.

34
Waterbury, Connecticut

IT HAD BEEN A LONG, FRUSTRATING WEEK FOR MEL
Pierce since Dr. Bethune had told him about the
Desmond Clinic, the only new angle in the case since
the Drayton debacle had become a dead end. After a
week of checking every medical organization and area
phone book, Pierce had found no trace of a clinic that
was now or had ever been called Desmond. He had no
other leads. No other ideas.

Then the phone call had come from Horace Bethune. The doctor's earlier gruff tone had entirely
disappeared, and he seemed eager to correct a mistake
he'd made. It turned out the association Bethune had
used to remember the name of the clinic was incorrect,
and an old record had jogged his memory further. The
name of the clinic was the same as a singer he and his
wife had liked, but the singer was Jerry Vale, not
Johnny Desmond. By the time the elderly ophthalmol-
ogist had begun apologizing, Pierce was already
thumbing through a telephone book.

*   *   *

The recently renovated Vale Memorial Medical Library was a starkly-modern building, encased by silver reflective glass that mirrored its surroundings. The organization had been set up in the 1950s by the Connecticut Association of Practicing Physicians as a centralized storehouse of medical treatment techniques that could be drawn upon by any accredited doctor in the state. The idea was novel then, but by the 1980s, many such libraries existed on both the state and national levels.

At five-thirty, when Pierce arrived at the antiseptic headquarters, most of the staff had already gone home. It was only with luck that he spotted an employee leaving the main entrance. The woman was young and pretty, and listened to Pierce's request politely. Patty Silverman, a local graduate student working part-time at the library as a researcher, had the presence of mind to ask to see his badge. Then she checked with her supervisor before giving him access to the files. She put Pierce on the line, and he instructed the director to check him out with the Milbrook Police if he felt it necessary. About ten minutes later, the phone rang and Patty Silverman listened to the brief message without any change in expression.

"So what is it you want to see?" she asked with an impressed sort of smile when she put down the receiver.

"Sometime in the 1960s, a gynecologist named Kreuger, John Kreuger, left some of his records to the Vale Medical Library. I'm hoping there's something about the doctor or his son."

216

In a short time they were in a high-ceilinged room filled with files that stacked to eye-level. In the center of the room was a small cubicle with a solitary chair and desk on which a projection unit rested.

"If we have what you're looking for, you'll find it under the doctor's name, or, if not, the specialty he practiced. Also we have a file cross-referenced to patients. Anything more than that requires some technical knowledge, you know, certain medical procedures and terms."

Pierce smiled briefly. "You're talking to a cop, remember? I'll try the first way, first."

"Okay," she said, returning his smile, "I'll get you John Kreuger's file, first."

An hour and a half later, eyes weary from squinting at all the Kreuger microfilm, Pierce had found nothing useful. He cranked the microfilm records one more position forward and suddenly the format was different. The formal records were gone and now, apparently, he was into a section of haphazard notes. At least it looked that way to him.

"They filmed everything?" he asked.

Patty stifled a yawn and nodded. "If he gave the library a grocery list it'll probably be there."

Pierce adjusted the rear projection light and the focus, which had changed with the smaller, harder-to-read, written notes. He clicked forward and found insurance documents, and then a detailed chronological record of what appeared to be Kreuger's own illness. The last entry on that page was a single word, *terminal*.

He moved forward again, anticipation growing.

There was a list, handwritten, that detailed personal
effects, the kind a parent might make up for a child
who was going somewhere, an extended vacation or
camp. And heading the list was the name Theodore,
the name on the watch! The long column of items
included articles of clothing, personal possessions and
a separate section on medicines with two of the five
medicines checked. The drugs all had exotic names
Pierce did not recognize. Then, under a heading la-
beled "jewelry," Pierce found an entry described simply as *gold watch*.

"What are these lines?" Pierce immediately asked,
pointing to two connecting parallel strokes at the top
of the list.

Patty Silverman moved closer to him, her perfume
faint in the air, saw what he was pointing at and
promptly giggled. "That's from a paper clip, silly.
Something else was attached to that page."

"Where would it be?"

"Try the next slide," she said, aware that Pierce was
deadly in earnest.

The next few film strips seemed unrelated to a child,
but then he was again staring at a page of scribbling
that had the same kind of paper-clip shadow at the top.
About halfway down, in a clutter of notes, was the
name and address of a couple, boxed off separately by
heavily-darkened, hand-drawn lines. It was near the
bottom of a list of other couples and their addresses,
all of whom had been crossed out. Next to the boxed-
off couple was a single check mark.

Finally, Pierce thought, finally I've got a break.

He quickly wrote down the boxed name and address. His eye scanned the rest of the page, and once again he moved the microfilm forward, this time finding a blank screen.

"That's the end of the file," Patty offered.

For an instant Pierce stared at the blank space, then suddenly backtracked to the last page. Something had caught his eye, registered and then was gone. He started at the top of the page again, looking through a long list of female names, presumably patients. Three-quarters of the way through the fifty-name list, he saw it: J. Jaison.

Pierce let out his breath slowly, knowing only that the Julie Weston case was about to become a great deal more complicated. The *J.*, he knew, was for Julie. And the *Jaison* was the last name from her first marriage.

"Did you find what you were looking for?" Patty Silverman asked with schoolgirl curiosity.

Pierce sat stock-still, staring at the hand-written letters. "Yes," he said softly, "I sure as hell did."

35
Wilton, Connecticut

PIERCE FOUND THE SLEEPY, PEACEFUL BLOCK WITH-out difficulty. He looked at the modest house that was Mr. and Mrs. Martin Cantrell's home and could not help thinking how dramatically their lives were about to change. And how, once again, his job as a detective would evoke hostility and, probably, fear.

Sad-eyed Ellen Cantrell opened the door, and after Pierce had identified himself, she let him in without a word. Pierce found that curious. Most people would have demanded to know the reason for a cop's visit before admitting him. Mrs. Cantrell was in her mid- to late-forties and had succumbed only in small ways to the normal artifices of a woman her age. There was no paint on her nails, almost no makeup on her face; plentiful gray decorated her hair; she dressed plainly and spoke the same way. Pierce found himself liking her immediately. It wouldn't make things any easier.

"I assume it's important if you came all the way from New York," she said timorously.

"Yes, I'm afraid it is. I don't want to alarm you, but someone's life may depend on what you can or can't tell me."

"How could something like that have anything to do with me?" she said quickly.

"Well, I didn't mean you, specifically."

She braced at his remark and Pierce immediately sensed that Ellen Cantrell knew, at least on some level, perhaps unconscious, what he was talking about.

"Maybe someone in your family. You do have a husband? And children?"

She nodded sharply. "You're making me very nervous. I think you should wait for my husband to get home. He'll be here pretty soon."

"Sorry," Pierce said, "I can't wait for his arrival, it's that important. No one thinks, Mrs. Cantrell, that you or your husband has done anything wrong. It's just that you may have information that will help us."

"What made you come here? How did you get our names?"

"Does the name Dr. John Kreuger mean anything to you?"

Ellen Cantrell's expression went from sad to hopeless in the wink of an eye.

"It would go back fifteen years or more," Pierce said gently, consciously giving the woman a moment to compose herself.

A car's tires crunched on the pebbled driveway and Ellen Cantrell said, almost inaudibly, "My husband."

When Martin Cantrell entered the house his wife threw him a worried glance that both he and Pierce saw clearly and neither acknowledged. After a quick explanation from Pierce, the couple excused themselves and conferred in private in an adjoining room.

"What do you want?" Martin Cantrell said shortly. "What's going on?"

Pierce plunged in. "Your names appeared on a list Dr. Kreuger made up around the time that he abandoned his practice. You were only one of several names on that list, but the only ones not crossed off. The question is—why?"

Martin Cantrell looked at his wife, then back at Pierce. "I don't think we have to answer that. It's a very private matter and I don't see . . . "

"You might not have to answer me," Pierce broke in harshly, "but you'll have to talk to someone. And soon. If you don't want to cooperate after I've told you how important it is, I'd have to ask myself why."

Ellen Cantrell's eyes darted around the room like a trapped animal's, and suddenly she looked as though she were about to cry. "Does this concern anyone besides us?" she managed to get out.

Pierce nodded quickly. "How old is your son, Mrs. Cantrell?"

"Twenty-one. Almost." She paused again. "I didn't tell you we had a son."

"I know you didn't."

"Would you mind telling me how your names got to be on Dr. Kreuger's list?"

"What do you think he's done?" Mr. Cantrell broke in.

"It will be easier if you answer my questions," Pierce said, not unkindly. He did not want to hurt these people. What he was going to do was a part of his job he did not enjoy.

"Dr. Kreuger was our son's real father," Cantrell volunteered resignedly.

"Was?"

"He's dead."

"And you adopted his son?"

Mrs. Cantrell nodded. "We wanted our own children but weren't successful. We asked a family friend to help us investigate a private adoption. We didn't want to go through an agency or anything like that because it took too long."

"And then?"

"Our friend helped, and before long we got a call from a lawyer. The lawyer said he represented someone who wanted to find a home for a young boy. He asked us to come to his office for an interview, but cautioned that we were just one of a number of couples he was meeting. Anyway, we did it.

"It took a long time, but I guess a lot faster than an agency would have taken. We waited about six months before being told we were the ones they'd chosen and were asked to go to an address in Ridgefield. In the meantime I found out someone was investigating us. Whoever it was called our bank, both our employers, even our church."

"The address turned out to be Dr. Kreuger's house?"

Both of the Cantrells nodded. Then Martin Cantrell took over. "We never met the man until the day we took Theodore home with us. We were told Dr. Kreuger was dying of some rare sickness, and all he cared about was selecting a good mother and father for his son." He looked at his wife and smiled wanly.

"Does your son still go by the name Theodore?"

"Yes," Mrs. Cantrell said quickly, "never Teddy or any nickname. Never."

"And he's lived with you ever since?"

"Yes," Mrs. Cantrell said and suddenly she was crying.

"What is it?" Pierce asked.

"Theodore isn't a normal boy," Martin Cantrell said, "never was. We knew that when we adopted him."

Through her tears, Ellen Cantrell sobbed, "We haven't seen him in almost a week." And the tears came harder.

"He's done this kind of thing before, disappearing without telling us where. But he's always come back before this long."

"We're worried sick," he said.

"You say he isn't normal. In what way?"

Martin Cantrell hesitated. "This probably won't mean anything to you, but the medical name for it is Routella Syndrome. It's a chemical and psychological disorder . . ."

"No one is sure what it is," his wife interrupted.

"Anyway, he gets spells, like attacks of anger. Sometimes it's expressed outwardly, often verbally, and sometimes he just gets sullen for days at a time." He drilled Pierce, suddenly, with a determined look. "But never violent. Never."

"Is it treatable?"

"There are physical disorders, spasms, nervous tics, and for a long time we had them under control with drugs, but lately . . ." His voice trailed off.

"We've been to dozens of specialists, but there's nothing anyone can do," his wife added mournfully. "There is no cure. Not really."

Martin Cantrell leaned forward, the determined look still in his eyes. "But let me tell you something about Theodore. I don't think there's a smarter kid in the state. He can outthink most people I know, and he's never had a teacher who didn't think he was brilliant. Another thing," he said, his hand in the air. "There isn't a mean bone in his body. He never hurt anyone in his life, and if he ever . . . ever went off the deep end, the danger would be the harm he'd do to himself. He's suffered a long time with his sickness,

224

and to be truthful I think lately he's given up hope."
He leaned closer to Pierce. "Can you even imagine
what it must be like? Being so different all your life?
Being an outcast. You know kids," he said, his voice a
mixture of anger and resignation, "they can be cruel,
very cruel."

"He wouldn't hurt anyone," Mrs. Cantrell repeated.

"He may already have," Pierce said evenly.

"He never even had a chance!" her husband blurted
out.

"Do you have a picture of Theodore anywhere?"

The Cantrells looked at one another and then Mr.
Cantrell got up and stalked out of the room. When he
returned he pushed a photo at Pierce.

"It's the best we have. It was taken a year or two
ago and it's not very good."

"Theodore doesn't like his picture taken," his wife
said. "He's a very private kind of person."

Pierce studied the photo. It showed a surprised-
looking kid of about seventeen, standing against a car.
He was tall and thin, his hair medium-long and very
blond. The shot wasn't very clear, but clear enough to
see the boy looked a lot like his own nephew, the boy
the Radio City guard had picked out of the lineup.

"I think it's time you left us alone," Martin Cantrell
said firmly.

Pierce looked at him and said nothing. Ellen Cantrell's soft weeping remained the only sound in the
room.

"Please," her husband said.

"I'm afraid this picture only makes it more likely

that Theodore is the boy we're looking for. Is there anything you can tell me about where he might be? For his own good, and yours. I have reason to believe he's going to do something, and soon."

"Do what?" Martin Cantrell demanded.

"If it does turn out that your boy is the one we're looking for, he might be trying to kill someone."

"Who the hell do you think you are, anyway?" a suddenly enraged Martin Cantrell shouted. "You don't know anything about us. You're guessing about things you don't know."

Pierce waited for the man's anger to wear off. He'd seen similar reactions many times before and knew calm was the best response.

He began softly. "I don't want to be cruel. But please try to think about what's happening. Obviously you've had some kind of trouble with Theodore before. If there's even a remote chance your boy is involved, it's going to go a lot worse for him if we can't help him fast. You can see that, can't you?"

Pierce did not tell them that their son had already murdered, that only tragedy awaited him. "There's one more thing I'd like to ask. It would help confirm whether or not Theodore may be involved." He pulled out a small manila envelope from his pocket. "Can you tell me anything about this watch?" He held it out in his palm and studied the Cantrells' faces. Instantly he knew they would not have to answer any more questions. Pierce saw from their expressions that suddenly, irrevocably, their faint hopes had been defeated. Martin Cantrell stood and faced Pierce squarely, the fight gone from him in one quick gust.

"What else can we tell you . . . that might help? We'll do anything."

"I appreciate that," Pierce said. He looked out the window where the afternoon light was dying and knew he was losing precious time.

"The only thing you might have been able to tell me is the one thing you really don't know. Where he is."

There was more silence until a weary Ellen Cantrell rose slowly from the sofa.

"No, we can't tell you that. If only we knew, ourselves. But there is something you probably should know . . . or see, that is. Maybe it will help; I don't know, but it's the only thing I can think of, now."

She turned away from Pierce to face her husband, who was biting his lower lip so hard it had turned white.

"The letter?" he said weakly.

She nodded, with pitiful, reddened eyes.

36
Wilton, Connecticut

THE BREAKING POINT WASN'T FAR AWAY. HE wanted to run in and quickly get what he needed, but instead he stalked his own house with the caution of a burglar. When he drew closer, the quiet reassured him, as did the empty two-car garage. It told him both *his parents were away. Just to make sure, he slipped around to the backyard and peered into the windows. Satisfied, he used his own key to enter, but found the back door already open, an oversight not typical of his mother's caution. It was evidence of her grief over his disappearance, and the thought made him guilty for a fleeting moment. But quickly he stopped that feeling; he had a job to do, a destiny to meet, and could not allow himself to be sidetracked by any feelings.*

Nothing could have brought him back except the pills. He'd not brought enough to the hideout. Normally he didn't have to worry about a big supply, but the past week hadn't been normal. The Cyclone had run almost every night and twice during the day, and he'd used up the last of them to keep from going completely off the tracks.

The stairs creaked under his weight. Outside, the sky was dark enough to rain, and as usual, the windows were shut and curtains drawn, so from the inside you could barely tell it was daytime at all. He paused at the top of the stairs to listen, but there were no sounds or lights coming from any of the rooms and no scent of the lemony perfume that would announce his mother's presence. But before going on he noticed the door to his own room was shut, and a few seconds later he heard the noise coming from inside.

The first sound was quickly followed by others— sounds of drawers being opened. His mind worked feverishly to understand who the intruder might be. If it was his mother, there would be tears and a fight as he got what he needed and left again; if it was his father, it would mean something a lot worse. But both

*their cars were gone, and the door to his room was
closed, so it had to be someone else.*

*The police were the next logical and frightening
guess. But how had they connected him to the murder
when they had the Drayton kid? He fought an urge to
scramble back down the stairs and escape, but he
needed the medicine and he needed it fast. Shaking
badly, he tiptoed down the hall to the window, opened
the venetian blinds, and looked out. The area in front
of the house was clear. Moving to one side of the
window, he gazed up the street and saw nothing, but
when he searched in the other direction he saw the
familiar black Lincoln and felt a cold hand clutching
at his belly. It was the car he'd seen with the old man
in it.*

*Carefully he walked back to his room, grasped the
metal doorknob, which felt oddly cold to the touch,
and turned it slowly. He waited, his mind racing, then
drew a deep breath and smashed his body into the
door.*

*The feeble old man was stooped over the desk when
the boy burst in with a thunderous crash. For a
moment he looked frightened enough to simply topple
over, but his hand snaked out and he steadied himself
on the desk. Once their eyes met, they both stopped
moving and stared at each other in unstated, mutual
recognition.*

"You know who I am?" the old man finally said.
His voice was weak, but, strangely, unafraid.

*The younger one kept staring at him in disbelief,
studying the aged face for a feature or a look that he
could recognize from memory. And he remembered*

the wrinkles. They were all over now—face, neck, hands. Once, he dimly recalled, he had tried to press those very wrinkles away.

"They told me . . . told me . . . you were dead." *His throat was closing and he suddenly wanted to vomit.*

The old man's eyes traveled over him as though he were an insect, a specimen to be studied.

"I'm sorry for that, Theodore," he said. "There were reasons, then. At that time it was better for you to believe it."

The youth took a belligerent step forward, but his legs stiffened and he went no further. He was confused. Everything had been so clear and now it was twisted. He needed the pills desperately. Soon it would be too late.

"I know what you did," *Theodore stammered. Both of his hands were already shaking uncontrollably.* "Everything."

"And I know what you have done," the old man answered calmly.

"It was in the letter. Damn you!" *he howled.*

"I am your father. I've come back to help you."

"I don't need anyone's help," *he shouted. His stomach was tightening and soon he wouldn't be able to breathe.*

The old man limped toward him, leaning on his cane. The metal tip made a noise that resonated dimly in the boy's mind. It was the same sound as the Cyclone clanking up the Big Hill.

"Don't come closer," *he yelled at the old man who continued to draw nearer.*

The rage was swallowing him up, making him blind.

230

The man blurred in his vision and he could now only see shapes of light and dark that stood for hair and flesh and clothing. Then one shape separated from the rest, and even in his confusion he knew it was the cane closing the distance between them.

"You've been watching me. Trying to stop me."

"I had to. Before you made it worse."

The whole room had begun to spin slowly. If he let himself pass out, it would be the end of everything he'd planned for all these months.

"It was my fault, not yours. That's why *I* had to stop you and no one else. Do you understand that? It's my fault."

Theodore tried frantically to comprehend what the man who called himself Father was saying, but it was all jumbled and nonsensical. His mind flooded with images, half-real, half-hallucination, that flowed maddeningly into one another. He saw himself in a large room with the father he remembered from childhood. There were books all around, hundreds of books. The chairs were crinkly leather and a blazing fire warmed him on one side of his face. Then the fire turned cold.

He stepped toward his father, wanting an explanation for what he was seeing. He saw the wrinkles getting closer and closer and he reached up to press them smooth. But when he touched the skin the features were someone else's and he recoiled when he recognized Artie Shore staring out at him from death, his life's blood pouring out of his back onto the polished wood floor. His eyes followed the stream of blood as it wrapped around his own feet and formed a bubbling pool. The surface of the blood became a mirror, and when he looked into it he saw not his own reflection but the beginning of a movie. The opening credits traveled up the blood-mirror and behind the indecipherable words a face was forming, a ghastly female face that leered at him as if he were the freak, not she.

A scream jarred him away from the face and suddenly the bloody mirror was retreating, shrinking before his eyes. His vision cleared, then honed in on the silver-tipped cane, again closing in on him. The sound was the clanking of the Cyclone, an all-too-familiar sound. The Cyclone, he knew, was hovering on the crest. Then it sprang forward and in a split-second all of the cars were hurtling down the steepest part of the Big Hill, racing at a thousand miles an hour and it was too late to get off.

"Let me help you," came the cry, but it was swallowed in the roar of the Cyclone and he did not have to listen to it any longer.

The cane closed the final distance between them. The passengers were screaming for their lives as two feeble arms reached out to encircle him. He could not feel them trembling as they held him in a tender grip. He could not sense the labored breathing. Raging inside, he reached for the cane and loosened it from the old man's grip with one sharp twist. He felt nothing at all as he raised it and brought it down onto the thin silver hair that came away in clumps, one, two, three times, until there was no movement in his victim, and never would be again. All he could hear were the screams of the passengers riding on the Cyclone as it hurtled off its tracks, spilling them out, end over end, toward oblivion.

It was too late for the pills. From that moment on, it would always be too late.

37
Danbury, Connecticut

AFTER HE'D CALLED TO INSTRUCT ROBERT MONT-gomery to stay at his office, Mel Pierce drove fast, back to Danbury. For one of the few times in his police career he had been surprised, no, flabbergasted, by the events of a case.

He was not sure, even now, whether he believed what was in the letter the Cantrells had given him. Normal walking-around-logic told him it was a fantastic story. Yet, incredibly, the facts of the case all fit together, the facts formed a pattern and the letter fit into that pattern.

He wheeled into the advertising agency's parking lot and half jogged into the office. He did not, any longer, want to be alone with what he knew.

"I'm going to give it to you all at once," Pierce said, launching into it. "I'm quite sure who the killer is. His name is Theodore Cantrell, he's twenty, and lives in Wilton. Does the name mean anything to you?" He waited for a sign of recognition that didn't come from Montgomery.

"You got him?" he asked eagerly instead.

"I've just been with his parents. They don't have any idea where he is; he's been missing for over a week."

Robert turned and slammed his fist into the wall. "Son of a bitch!" He spun toward Pierce. "You haven't told my wife, have you?"

"I alerted Rachel at the house, but told them not to tell her. Then I rushed right over here."

Robert sank heavily into his large desk chair. "Just so you know what's going on, Julie's doctor came again yesterday and was worried enough to discuss the possibility of a Caesarean section. Her pressure's up again, and he says it's touch and go from here on in. She can't take the waiting; it gives her too much time to think."

"We won't tell her anything if you don't want us to."

"From now on I'm staying with her myself, full-time," Robert said. "Does knowing who the murderer is really help us?"

Pierce shook his head. "Hard to say. He's loose and we don't know where. It might help. It might not."

"Jesus," Robert said.

"I have something to show you," Pierce began, taking out a handful of paper. "This explains a lot of things, especially why this psycho picked your wife. It turns out it's not random or connected to the movies or that he's ever likely to stop."

"What do you have?" Robert asked quickly.

234

"The missing link between the killer and the watch, and maybe everything else. It's a copy of a letter written twenty years ago by a dying father, to the couple who adopted his son. It was never supposed to be opened until the boy was older, but somehow he got his hands on it. Immediately afterwards, this whole thing with your wife started. I think it would be a good idea for you to read it *now*." Pierce shook his head. "But I'm telling you, you probably won't believe it."

Robert looked with surprise at Pierce. The detective's whole manner was completely different. He seemed unsure of himself, confused, and maybe even rattled.

"The strangest thing I've ever come across," Pierce was saying, "I swear it is." He handed Robert the papers.

Robert unfolded the first page and began to read the short introduction that preceded the main text. The handwriting was extraordinarily precise, painstaking. Whoever had written it had taken a lot of time.

> The following notes are a record of the unusual circumstances surrounding the birth of my son, Theodore Kreuger, on March 13, 1959. These facts have been kept a secret in the best interests of the child and exist only in the event they may become needed for emergency medical or psychological treatment.
>
> At the time of this writing, the medical community would no doubt strongly condemn the practice set forth herein, but it is my hope and belief by the time this record is revealed, an era of true

235

scientific investigation will have arrived. If, by then, there are those who still think me a mad and reckless scientist, then I fear for a society whose moral judgments continue to limit what may be achieved.

Robert looked up at Pierce only long enough to see his dour, perplexed expression hadn't changed; then he continued reading.

In addition to the research for which I am most known, I continue in my sizable gynecology practice for as many hours a day as a worsening illness permits. Throughout my pursuit of the healing arts I have enjoyed an elevated standing, both as physician and researcher. My office practice flourished due, in no small part, to the successful treatment of certain patients refused by others of my profession. I state this only to help those who may judge my actions to understand the context in which an extraordinary experiment was completed.

From the beginning, I found myself greatly at odds with some of the views held by the medical establishment. In the course of my counseling, therefore, it became impossible for me to ignore one kind of suffering for which unfeeling dogma prevented remedy. For all of my patients, the problem of unwanted pregnancy cast a dark shadow over their lives. At first I adhered to common practice and denied these women my comfort, but this was cowardly and done only out of concern for the repercussions which would follow what was, for me, an act of conscience. In time, however, I could no longer deny my beliefs, and, in cases of exceptional need, I began to provide the nurturing help for which I became a physician. For most of my patients, therapeutic abortion became the only alternative to humiliation or risk of injury at the hands of someone far less qualified to help them.

After performing hundreds of abortions I began work on an unorthodox experiment and became fascinated by an ultimate goal of my research. By that time my investigations into fetal structuring had received wide acclaim and grants and, together with my practice, provided the resources needed for further experimentation. I freely admit that I had come to think of myself as a renegade and felt unconstrained by convention.

The idea for the experiment came from my patients themselves, and soon became an obsession. Working as an abortionist, I was driven by the notion of saving one of the embryonic lives which I was "taking" on a daily basis. Soon every waking thought was devoted to this one, glorious possibility, and before long, I selfishly limited my practice to those patients whose personal problems could advance my work.

The time that followed was a living torture of expectation and defeat until one day I succeeded at prolonging embryonic life outside its mother.

The long-sought result lasted for only a few minutes, but the success compelled me forward and was followed by many more until one embryo endured for more than six hours.

Robert stopped reading and looked up at Pierce. "What in God's name am I reading?"

"Just keep going, Robert," Pierce answered, and something in the detective's voice sent a cold shiver up Robert's spine.

For months afterwards, I barely slept or ate as I carried on my work alone, for fear of a betrayal by even the most trusted ally. I knew it was a matter of time until I perfected the right combination of incubation, nourishment and maternal continuity.

From the beginning, I assumed the need for as full-grown an embryo as could safely be removed from its mother. The more the fetus could develop naturally, the less precarious the tender life when it was no longer being serviced by nature. As my research reached a critical stage, I was visited by a woman whose case history satisfied the three criteria I had established. She and her fetus showed every sign of good health, she was in her twentieth week, and her need for discretion was almost as extreme as my own. Although married, she implored me to keep the abortion secret from her husband, from whom she'd been able to hide the fact of her pregnancy. When I agreed, the operation took place without incident, and the woman left my office believing it an end to the matter. (The patient's complete medical history is enclosed.)

A thin line of sweat ran down Robert's side as he thumbed through the pages of the medical workup, one of two lengthy enclosures.

"Is this what I think it is?" he said incredulously.

Pierce stared back at him and said nothing.

Robert saw the name John Kreuger several times in the text before coming to the case history of the woman. The name at the top of the workup was Julie Jaison and below, there was a small picture of her.

Robert gulped, trying to catch his breath and slow his suddenly wild heartbeat. A silent minute went by, and another. "It would kill her to know about this," he said finally, and Mel Pierce thought he'd never heard a sadder voice in all his life. "It seems . . . seems just . . ."

"Unbelievable," Pierce finished. "I know," he said softly.

Robert tried to imagine the conditions which had led to Julie's request for an abortion in the first place. Given the way she now felt about having a baby, it was something difficult to fathom. He also thought how impossible it was to truly know another person, even a wife or husband, how impossible it was to truly be in another's shoes.

"Mr. Montgomery," Pierce broke in, "keep going. Please."

"All right," Robert answered.

The male fetus was removed intact and survived for twenty-two hours before the first crisis. There was a sudden cessation of breathing that seemed irreversible until I applied a series of mild electric shocks, and the fetus, no larger than my hand, responded favorably. The same phenomenon occurred twice more during the first week, but each time ending with a miraculous regeneration of the life force. I almost began to feel as though I could exercise the power of creation, and perhaps it was true. After the fourth week, the interruptions of breathing stopped and the embryo began to grow normally. The success confirmed my "blasphemous" theory that once begun, the life process could be continued ex utero by surrogate.

In truth, I expected the experiment to fail. Insurmountable problems of nutrition, rejection, hostile environment and others of which I wasn't even aware, any one or in combination, should have taken their inevitable toll. But for unknown reasons, in this instance the power of life proved more durable than I had dared to believe. The fetus not only lived, but it thrived in my laboratory. Suspending my normal practice entirely, I continued to devote myself to the singular end of maintaining the fragile life I had resurrected. At first I had planned to share my discovery with medicine and thereby force a break in the conventions I so loathed. The enclosed accounts of my procedures were kept meticulously for this purpose. But as my fetus took on humanity I was quickly confronted by a powerful influence I had no way to anticipate. By the time the fetus was taken away from the life-supporting apparatus and had grown into a normal infant, a bonding relationship had already begun between us, and it was this humanity which first delayed and later negated my decision to share the discovery with the world outside. To have done so would not only have taken him from me but turned him into a freak forever.

Maintaining the secret of his birth until the body had grown, I enlisted a succession of nurses and together we raised the boy I named Theodore, after my own father. The boy was raised to believe I was his natural father, his real mother having died in childbirth. To the best of my knowledge, this is what he still believes. Later, after learning of my own deteriorating condition, the papers necessary for adoption were created.

There appears to be only one negative and lasting effect of the boy's unnatural birth, and as of this writing I am greatly disturbed by what I have observed. Although there is no way to know with certainty, it is possible that during the interruptions of breathing in the incubation stage, the flow of oxygen was stopped long enough to damage the brain. Whether this explains the sporadic episodes of neurological trauma from which Theodore suffers, I do not know for certain. These episodes have occurred from the age of four and take on many forms. The raging anger is the most frightening, because during these attacks the boy needs to be protected from himself. The change from a normally passive state may erupt at any time with wild screams and thrashing about, and is often attended by the foulest of language. During this time the body becomes afflicted with tics and spasms and a range of muscular irregularities. Unaffected intellectually by this affliction, the boy is aware of his suffering even in the midst of the seizures, and one can only speculate on the depth of the hell in which he finds himself. Mercifully, the extreme fits come infrequently, and more often take the form of depression and feelings of loneliness. Most of the case sufferers of the Syndrome are young males, and it has been determined that many possess enough control over their affliction to suppress symptoms for varying lengths of time until the inevitable emotional explosion. It saddens me to think that the child suffers even more than I have witnessed, but controls it, perhaps for my benefit. Thus far, the affliction has been treated with strong drugs, and the lasting effect of these medicines is unknown.

After long investigation, I have found the boy's symptoms correspond in almost every way with a sickness that has come to be known as Routella Syndrome. This is a biochemical disorder resulting in brain-wave abnormalities which can cause an interruption of signals to the body. One in ten thousand is affected by this disorder to some degree; thus, there is no way for me to know if it was his unusual birth that caused it or if it occurred spontaneously, as it does in others.

In all other ways, Theodore appears to be a normal, healthy and extraordinarily intelligent child. Had fate been more generous to us, perhaps we might have lived out the cycle of our lives in relative contentment. But the cruel and progressive disease with which I now suffer has forced me to seek another home for the boy before he is again left parentless. It is to this effort that I have dedicated the last of my strength.

The letter was signed "John M. Kreuger, M.D., June 1, 1965."

After allowing Robert to collect himself, Pierce pulled the papers away from him.

"It looks like there was another page that came before the medical data. They were all numbered, and they skip from four to six."

"What do you think was on it?"

"A good guess might be some kind of personal note, to the boy himself. When the real adoption took place, this letter was given to the new parents with the condition the boy might read it when he turned twenty-one."

Robert was shaking his head, his thoughts already with Julie and what it would be like for her to learn the murderer stalking her was a son she never knew she had, the product of a fantastic experiment more than twenty years earlier.

"One of the reasons I think the missing page was a personal message, was in the kid's room itself. I've

just come from there. Among other things I found
some burnt paper that could have been that page. Now
it's only ashes."

"You mean that . . . that *he* read the letter? He
knows everything that's in there?"

"Yes. How else would he have known about your
wife? We believe he read the original letter in his New
York doctor's office, an office which he then de-
stroyed. Right after that incident, this whole thing got
started. With a little research, the kid could have
easily tracked down Julie Jaison to the present day,
right through the name changes. Plus, he had the
snapshot to go on. And it wasn't as if Julie's face was
hard to find. It was on movie posters all over the
country."

"*Mommy,*" Robert said, "it explains *Mommy.* And
why he hates her . . . for trying to . . ." Robert stopped
in mid-sentence, "for trying to get rid of him."

Pierce nodded grimly and said nothing.

38
Milbrook, Connecticut

BEFORE THE CALL HAD COME, A STRONG FOREBODING
had descended over her, a premonition that something
terrible was about to happen. Nearly at the same time
she also thought the painful onset of labor had finally
arrived. Without warning, a series of cramps forced

her legs up against her chest to ease the excruciating spasms; she was so sure it was labor, she called for Rachel and went over the memorized breathing technique in her mind. There were four or five more sets of cramps, just as strong, at regular intervals after which, unaccountably, they stopped.

When Rachel left, the nausea persisted and the feeling of being cut off and alone became more unbearable than ever. So, when the phone rang at a few minutes after five, her resolve not to answer gave way to the longing to connect with Robert, or someone, and she reached for the receiver. But by the time she'd picked up, someone else, not Robert, was talking to Rachel, and she thought it was Pierce saying, "Don't take any chances now." That was when another severe cramp hunched her over and she felt her courage drain. She dropped the phone back into its cradle, trapped between not wanting to know what was going on and needing to know.

The second call changed everything. It came at five-thirty-five, well after Robert should have been home. By then, there was no doubt in her mind it was he, and without hesitation, and against orders, she picked it up.

"Mommy? Is that you, Mommy?"

The second she heard the voice, she felt a scream rising in her. *It was He. He was still out there. Waiting.* She stifled the scream and held onto the phone.

"Just Mommy and me, and her baby-to-be." The voice was singing, and when it stopped, the words were replaced by a wet, slobbering kind of laughter.

She ordered her hand to put the phone down, but an insane fascination prevented it from moving.

"Who . . . who is this?" she managed to struggle out. "What do you want from me?"

There was silence on the other end and for an instant she didn't know which frightened her more, that the creature was still there—or that he was gone. Desperately, she hoped that Rachel had picked up, listening for anything that might be a clue.

"Just Mommy and me, and her baby-to-be," the voice sang out again.

The laughter that followed was grotesque and inhuman; Julie started to cry out to the others, but stopped herself. Maybe they were already listening and not telling her. It would be easy, she knew, to hang up, but smarter and braver not to.

She closed her eyes and endured it.

"Mommy had a little boy His hair was white as snow. But Mommy said I want him dead and why I'll never know."

Julie forced her attention away from the crazy, meaningless rhymes. She told herself he couldn't hurt her, that she should try to get to him, somehow, catch him off-guard and make him say something revealing.

Don't think about what he's saying. Think of the answer. Please God, let me say the right thing.

"I'm sorry . . . if I . . . hurt you," she said. "Can you forgive me?"

The line went deadly quiet, and for a second she thought he'd hung up. She was about to try it again when a small child's sing-song chanting cut her off.

"Roses are red, violets are blue. You kill me, now I kill you."

Keep it going, she commanded herself against the powerful instinct to slam down the phone. *You might have gotten to him.* The terror was still within her, but she was suddenly feeling slightly more in control of it.

"You can still be my little boy . . . if you want to. It's not too late." She spoke softly, imitating the sound of love.

"Baby makes three. Baby makes three," the voice now screamed back. She'd made him angry. There was no logic to it.

"What's your name? Tell me your name and maybe I can remember."

Now he was singing again, crooning *Lullaby and Goodnight* to her. But behind the singing, at first far in the background, then nearer and nearer, she could make out a grotesque counterpoint to the lullaby. It was a woman's screams, urgent and panicky, as though she was being attacked. Then the screams were familiar, and it came to her with revulsion. They were her own screams from the movie. Somehow the maniac must have recorded them from the film and put it together on a tape with the song to produce a chilling effect.

"Stop it!" Julie could not help herself from yelling. "Stop it! I'm not your mother. Leave me alone!"

His laughter rose above the cacophony behind it, and then, suddenly, almost instantly, the voice was calm again. It started up low and dirge-like, perfectly controlled:

"Now I lay me down to sleep, I pray the Lord my soul to keep. Mother and child I come to take, Tonight you'll die before you wake."

Julie stiffened with horror. This last was the worst. He was coming for her, coming for her baby. Without knowing why she believed him, she knew with all her heart he could do it and no one could stop him. Her whole body began to tremble and her stomach heaved upward.

The line went dead.

39
Danbury, Connecticut

AFTER RACHEL'S CALL ROBERT VICIOUSLY SLAMMED the phone down. The worst thing that could possibly have happened, Julie's being reached on the phone by the murderer, had happened. Lonely, scared, depressed, Julie had simply picked up the telephone. She had been expressly instructed not to answer; that was Rachel's job, but she'd done it anyway.

The office was quiet now, at nearly six o'clock. After the unbelievable experience of reading the letter, Robert needed, he knew, a little time to himself. He had to decide what to tell Julie, if anything, and when to tell her. He'd placed a call to Bain, but the doctor's service had picked up, so he'd left a message, and frustrated, he sat at his desk, thinking about what he should do.

"We're at the end," Pierce had said before leaving to meet Mallor at the Montgomery house. Now, a half hour later, things looked even worse. The Kreuger story was totally mad, on its own, nearly too much for Robert to absorb, much less understand. Now the killer had reached Julie. He seemed to Robert, trapped in his own nightmarish fantasy, omnipresent, almost God-like in his ability to reach out and touch them, fouling and ensnaring them more deeply with each contact. "At the end," Robert muttered to himself, fighting a profound hopelessness.

Then he thought of Julie, lying in bed, waiting as she had waited over the long, agonizing months and he felt instantly ashamed of himself. No matter what he knew, no matter what happened next, he could not afford the feelings he had allowed, for the first time, to penetrate his iron-clad self-control.

His entire focus had to be on Julie, *it had to be,* and any other feelings were worthless and weak, and, he knew from instinct, *dangerous*.

Robert jumped up from his desk like a man who'd been touched by electricity. He snatched the car keys from the desk, and fled the office into the quiet hall. His heart pounding as though it would explode, he sprinted to the reception area.

The lobby was the last distance to cover before the parking lot. He was already planning the shortest, fastest route home, estimating how long it would take to get there, knowing it was suddenly the most important thing for Julie's safety to be with her *now*. Mallor was there, Pierce was there, but something else demanded *his* presence, and nothing else, even the illogic of it, mattered.

Up ahead, he saw a Federal Express boy, making his usual last-call pickup. He raced past the kid wordlessly, sensing him flinch as a crazed-looking executive flashed by.

Robert grabbed for the door, feeling his fingers circle the knob. Then, as if at a great distance, he heard the pop of a firecracker, and another, and suddenly his right shoulder was aflame. He cracked into the door, his movements suddenly spasmodic and uncontrollable, and twisting, he felt himself slump in slow motion, to the floor.

Uncomprehendingly, he looked up and saw the tall, blond Federal Express messenger standing at the reception desk, holding his hand out to him. The fire flashed down his right arm, burning white-hot. The messenger's face was utterly blank. A pistol appeared in his hand and suddenly Robert understood what had happened. And what was to happen. The gun sounded muffled this time; it stung him again and he clutched out at his own chest with stiffening fingers.

Black ink seemed to fill his eyes and his mind felt lazy and slow. He struggled to see his assailant through the ink, but now there were only darkening shadows and vague shapes in front of him. From a great distance, like an echo through a tunnel, Robert heard a voice whisper in his ear: *"Mommy and me and baby make three."*

Then there were dull, thudding steps reverberating away. He heard a scream and realized, dumbly, that it was his own. Then the heat balloon that seared his chest burst like a great fireball and the shadows grabbed out at him.

40
Danbury, Connecticut

HE FELT EXHILARATED. HIS BODY WAS SINEWY AND strong, his mood buoyant, as though all the world waited for him to command it. Driving slowly and carefully up the big hill to the hospital, his mind went triumphantly back to the victory at the office.

He could still see the weakling's eyes, spinning with fear, and the blooming red circle that spread across his dress shirt.

It had been quick. Simple. For a man with his killing skills and his cunning, it had been nothing more than stepping on a roach.

Now, there was the final plan to put into action. The beauty of that plan was that she would come to him. Flushed out of the house like a rat. The cops had underestimated his genius, he knew, and that mistake was going to cost them. And most importantly, cost her.

He had it all thought out, as before, except that this

was more complicated, more brilliant. His plans had been carefully conceived, step by step. And those steps would lead to Her.

Tonight she would be his. And there was nothing or anyone who could stop it.

41

Milbrook, Connecticut

"OH, MY GOD," MEL PIERCE MUTTERED AS HE LIS-
tened to the doctor from Danbury Hospital. "Jesus."
He felt the blood drain out of his face as the voice went
on. "All right," he said finally. "Yes. Thank you."

He put the phone down and turned back to the living
room, where Scotty Mallor, Rachel, and Casey waited
wordlessly.

"Robert's been shot," he said quickly, knowing
from sad experience there was no other way to say it
than saying it outright. "He's critical. It doesn't look
good."

He watched as Casey's beautiful face was instantly
transformed into a mask of grief. She stood stock-still
for perhaps ten seconds and then, suddenly, her legs
buckled and she stumbled forward. Rachel reached
out quickly and grabbed her at the waist; the girl,
sobbing quietly, turned and buried her face in the
black woman's broad shoulder.

"Where and when?" Mallor asked, successfully keeping the shock he felt out of his voice.

"Couldn't have been more than fifteen or twenty minutes after I left him," Pierce spat out. "In the office. Near the front door. He must have just been leaving. He'd wanted to stay by himself for a few minutes after I left. Just to collect himself."

Pierce's eyes averted Mallor, who understood what the other cop was feeling, understood the mixture of rage and frustration and helplessness which ate at his guts like acid and left him trembling and violent and utterly sick at heart. Mallor also knew there was only one feeble antidote to the feeling: keep going.

"What now, Mel?" he said gently. "What do we do?"

Pierce let the fire in him subside, aware that Mallor had said the right thing. The Connecticut cop was a good man. A good officer, and Pierce was glad to have him on his side.

Quickly, Pierce went through the latest developments. First, the phone call getting through to Julie, a call that implied—hell—*stated,* an immediate threat. Now, Robert Montgomery, shot and probably dying. "Tonight is it," Pierce said. "We've got to operate on that assumption."

All his life Mel Pierce had been unafraid to take action. If something is wrong, you do something about it. You take control—or try to, a small voice inside him whispered—rather than wait for events to unfold. If you make a mistake, especially one where a life is at stake, be sure it's a mistake of commission. Now was one of those times.

It was too dangerous for Julie to stay in the house. He'd decided it as soon as he'd heard about the call to her, and the decision became rock-hard with the news about Robert.

"Rachel," he said, "call Dr. Bain. At home."

The heavyset woman sprang up from the couch with surprising nimbleness and headed for the phone. "What do you . . . "

"We're moving Julie to the hospital," Pierce interrupted. "Have him make the arrangements. Tell him it's an emergency, and tell him why. When it gets dark, in about two hours, we're leaving. Actually," Pierce added to Mallor, "you're leaving."

"What's your idea?" Mallor asked.

"After this length of time I think the killer has to be operating on the assumption that Julie will stay in the house. Maybe even have the child here. He must know it's about time for her to deliver. He knows she's here, now. Tonight. So he's gotta be coming here."

"That makes sense. And the last phone call was really whacked out, slobbering and crying and singing. We're not dealing with a cool, master criminal, here."

"Exactly. He's gone around the bend. And we're gonna be waiting for him."

"You want help?"

"No, nothing that could signal that something's changed. Moundsey's outside, right?"

"Yeah. Out front."

"Good. We want this place to look exactly like it does on every other night. Our man shot Robert when everyone else in the office had gone home. I'm sure he

254

figured that no one would find him quickly. He even turned out the lights, and locked the office doors."

"What happened, then?"

"A writer came back to do some work for a morning meeting. He spotted a lot of blood on the reception room floor all the way from outside, and called the Danbury stationhouse without going in."

"And you figure the kid comes here next?"

Pierce nodded. "Don't know when, of course, depends on just how crazy he is. I would think he'd wait until the middle of the night."

"Or maybe until lights go out. Or someone leaves the house. Whatever might show that fewer people were around."

Pierce grinned without humor. "Yeah. That's why your car is taking Julie and you. We dress Julie in Rachel's clothing and off you go."

"You don't think he'll spot the trick?"

"I don't think so. We'll hide Julie's face. Plus, it's dark in the car. My car stays and he'll figure I'd never let her out of my sight."

"Right."

"Plus, this bastard is no shrinking violet. He's had nothing but success so far, and he's completely out of his mind, and that combination tells me he's overconfident, maybe careless, and ready to be taken."

"It makes sense," Mallor repeated, staring back at Pierce, wondering how long this idea had been forming in Mel's brain and how much he really believed it would work.

"It better," Pierce answered. "It's all I got."

* * *

255

He waited in the bushes as the sun deepened in color and began to fade. He was nervous, really nervous now, and shifted uncomfortably as rivulets of sweat worked down his back. He'd never done anything like this before. But he was angry. And embarrassed. He'd been humiliated and he couldn't take that. It wasn't right. He had to get even.

He watched from the thicket as the sun fell below the rise of hills, miles away. As promised, the envelope was in the jacket pocket—and what was in it. It was going to be safe, and easy.

All he had to do now was wait. Just wait. And do nothing.

42
Milbrook, Connecticut

"IT'S TIME."

Julie struggled to her feet when Sergeant Mallor's voice sounded through the door. She moved unsteadily, her legs weak from inactivity and unaccustomed to her ever-increasing weight.

"Lean on me," Rachel said, and gratefully Julie did so. She made it to the living room before needing a rest. The dark makeup on her face itched, and looking down at Rachel's flowered dress, which had had to be slit around the midriff, she thought, if Mother could only see me now. She looked up, expecting smiles on the others' faces, then realized she hadn't spoken out loud.

"I don't understand why Robert hasn't come home." She looked at Pierce and Mallor, who were wearing identically impassive expressions. Rachel averted her gaze. "Casey?" she said.

"Come on, Mom," Casey answered, more bravely than she, herself, had expected. "Detective Pierce says it's important to go now."

Casey's eyes, Julie saw, were red. And her voice had a tremor. "Casey?" she repeated, her own voice quickly sounding panicky and unsteady. "Casey, what's going on?" Julie had never felt in less control of her life than at that moment—had never felt weaker, less capable of "handling things." She needed Robert now, more than she had ever needed anyone. And that's when she knew.

"Casey?" she shouted again. Almost instantly, she saw her daughter start to sob softly, and Julie felt a shock-wave of dread go through her limbs. Numb, and suddenly deathly-cold, she stared at Casey through a narrowing, sepia-toned field of vision.

"Mrs. Montgomery," Pierce said firmly, his voice penetrating the mist gathering in her mind, "you've got to leave, now."

She felt Sergeant Mallor grip her left elbow and Casey her right. "What's happened to Robert?" She asked it three more times before she realized it was better not to know and she allowed them to take her away.

* * *

Mel Pierce came out the back door of the kitchen, walked carefully through the backyard in an apparent sweep of the grounds, then slowly turned down the driveway and headed for the street where Moundsey was waiting. While he walked, he deliberately looked left and right and back again, for all the world appearing to do the nightly perimeter check.

"All right," he said tersely to the young, obviously nervous patrolman, "let's do it." They were now completely out of sight of the snug house behind them, and the street was as dark and silent as the leaves hanging like a million limp hands from the trees. As arranged, they took off at a brisk pace down the road for half a mile, past the end of the Montgomerys' property, and stopped for a breather before entering the woods and circling in behind the family's acreage.

Moundsey, three years past his high school football stardom, looked as if he was about equal to the exertion, but Pierce felt as though a weight were pressing on his chest.

Nerves, he knew, could make you dead-weary, no matter what kind of shape you were in.

"Sorry," the young man said, his hands pressing around his hips. "Give me a minute?"

"Take your time," Pierce said in a whisper. "I know how you feel."

"Yeah."

"We're not in a rush. We're doing this whole thing slow and easy." Pierce dropped to his haunches, balanced on his toes, and stared into the woods, consciously slowing and balancing his own breathing.

"Okay," Moundsey whispered a few minutes later,

and they entered the woods, moving parallel to the western edge of the Montgomery property.

Almost ten careful minutes later, they were deep in the woods behind the back line of the property, and ready to turn right and move parallel to the road, so they would be well in back of the house. A few minutes later, they were in behind the house, on the opposite side of the steep, sloping hill which blocked the house lights. "Okay," Pierce whispered, "when we get to the top we'll have a clear line of sight to the house. If someone's out here my guess is they'll be somewhere on the other side of the hill, down the slope."

"Okay," Moundsey gulped.

"Even at the top of the hill, we're a long way off, about two hundred yards, so if our boy's out here he'll certainly be between us and there."

"Right."

They crept quietly higher and at the crest, Pierce put a hand on Moundsey's shoulder and they stopped. The house glowed brightly down the hill and across a meadow, lit up, room by room, as every night.

Pierce put his finger to his lips and shook his head. Moundsey nodded, hesitated, then pointed at his gun. Pierce blinked his approval, and the patrolman slid the weapon out of its holster.

They waited, unmoving, searching the land that dropped off below them.

As they remained motionless, the night seemed to close in on them, close and unpleasantly warm. The scent of decay, faint yet distinct, filled the air, catching Pierce by surprise. He'd always thought the lush Connecticut hillside would have a clean, foresty smell, but now it seemed more like the stagnation of the Jersey meadowlands, an endless cycle of growth, death, and rot that warm summer evenings near the swamps always conjured.

Pierce felt acute, his senses keen and preternaturally tuned. He smelled the sharp odor of fear from the boy next to him and wished it was Mallor, instead. This kid might not be dependable. That was bad. But now, it was too late.

With a single motion of his hand, they started off, working slowly, very slowly, down the hill. Ten yards and stop. Wait. Listen. Then another ten yards, until, when the distance between them and the house had closed by almost half, they heard the distinct sound.

The disturbance started with the closing of a car door in the Montgomery driveway. Even from that distance the mechanical sound rang out with crystal clarity in the quiet woods. It was time for the planned escape, which was off to a noisier start than Pierce had planned.

When the two men heard the startling slap of metal on metal, it froze them in their tracks for the few seconds before they heard the other noise, this one closer to them and below their line of sight. It was the light, but unmistakable sound of wood splintering, either from an animal, or a man in the blackness around them. If it was a man, possibly he had been caught off-guard, as they were, by the beginning of the escape.

Instantly, Pierce's hand went to Moundsey's shoulder, and they stopped. Pierce strained his eyes toward the sound. There was another rustle. He slid his own gun out of his shoulder holster and felt Moundsey tense next to him.

Could it be an animal, Pierce thought. And were they about to blow their cover on a false alarm?

There was another rustle. Pierce's heart picked up its beat. This is it, he thought, and fought himself to go slow.

The sound was below them and to the left, perhaps thirty yards away. They moved straight across the hill, above the sound, on hands and knees now, barely inching along.

The rustle came again and suddenly, with all his heart, Pierce knew it was a man down there, not a deer, or a raccoon, or a woodchuck. They stopped directly above, from where the disturbance had last come. Another, larger twig snapped then, off to the left, and another. It was moving, away from the house, up the hill. That didn't make any sense, unless they had been spotted and the kid was in flight.

And then he saw him—saw a swatch of blond hair and a dark body below. Pierce felt the hair rise on the back of his neck. The blond swatch disappeared, but the underbrush kept telling the story, and as though he'd suddenly lost his sense of direction, he was coming toward them, now.

Pierce tensed, his arms quivering in anticipation. He did not move, holding himself absolutely rigid. He heard Moundsey swallow behind him and shift his weight.

The moment they'd been praying for was at hand. Pierce rose silently to a half-crouch, leaned behind to push a finger into Moundsey's knee to alert him, and slipped his index finger around the trigger of his gun. A flash not more than ten yards away sent him into action.

"Police!!" he shouted. "Stop where you are!!" He felt Moundsey rise up behind him and, in a corner of his mind, something said that it was all wrong.

The dark figure rose out of a thicket like a ghost, stood still, and then, suddenly, the right hand was moving and something glinted in the moonlight.

"Watch out!!" Pierce bellowed.

Without warning Moundsey's revolver went off behind him with a deafening explosion and instantaneously there was a scream.

And then it was quiet again. There were no night sounds, no birds, no crickets. Moundsey was down next to him breathing in spurts on Pierce's neck. "I saw a gun," he said. "I think I hit him."

They waited. There was nothing.

Pierce crawled sideways along the hill, until he could see through an opening in the thick bush and could make out the silhouette of the downed boy. The blond head was not moving. He stood up. "Be careful," he said. They walked slowly, carefully, toward the prone figure, guns drawn. Five feet away Pierce saw the body was sprawled face down. There was an unlit flashlight in his right hand.

At that instant he sensed something terrible.

He reached the still figure, leaned down and rolled him over on his back.

The blank eyes of Billy Drayton stared back up at him.

"My God in heaven," Pierce whispered.

"Billy?" Moundsey mumbled in disbelief.

Pierce reached down to check the boy's pulse. There was none. Pierce took the flashlight, shining it on the face, then worked it lower. Two green pieces of paper that protruded from a shirt pocket turned out to be two crisp, new hundred-dollar bills. In a moment he removed a white envelope from the kid's trouser pocket, pulled it out, and held it under the light.

"Detective Melvyn Pierce" was neatly typed on the envelope.

Pierce's heart thumped hard. The poor dumb bastard, he thought. The real killer had gotten to him again, this time for good. He tore open the envelope. Inside there was a single sheet of inexpensive, lined composition paper, the kind school kids used, the kind on which all the killer's notes had been written. He unfolded the paper with trembling fingers.

There was one word on it, scrawled childishly in red crayon: *"Surprise!"*

43
Danbury, Connecticut

THE MATERNITY WING OF DANBURY HOSPITAL wasn't a wing at all, but rather the fifth floor of the hospital's spanking-new, nine-story tower. The modern glass and steel structure was built adjacent to the old brick hospital. The two radically different buildings were joined together for four floors, at which point the new tower rose alone five more stories, affording patients on the higher floors a splendid panorama of the nearby rolling hills.

An unfortunate effect for the patients on the south side of the fifth floor was the old hospital, which stretched directly out from beneath their windows and offered a lovely view of heating ducts, vents, and two blackened chimneys. More than once during the repair of the existing building, workmen had scared the daylights out of patients in bed by simply strolling past their windows at eyeball-to-eyeball level. Julie Weston Montgomery's room, 531, was on the south side of the new tower.

*   *   *

At 10:45 P.M., Scotty Mallor sat tilted back in a chair outside room 531. He had heard nothing from Rachel back at the house yet, which did not surprise him; it only made sense that the killer would wait until later at night. A time that, in a mystery novel, a genre to which Mallor was addicted, would be called "the dead of night." Funny, Mallor thought for an instant, that both Julie and her husband would end up in the same hospital on the same night—or maybe that's the way the murderer had planned it, to be sure Julie was there.

Casey was in the room with her mother. At the last minute, she'd persuaded the officer to let her go along, and after all that had happened, he couldn't say no. Julie was asleep now, exhausted from a series of cramps that had come and then gone thirty-five minutes ago. After being told about Robert, Julie had also been given a strong sedative. She was told he was critical and could not be seen, though he was on the floor below. The maternity wing was quiet and subdued at this hour, as though the babies-to-be knew it was best to wait through the night before making their "entrances."

Mallor watched a blond nurse move purposefully down the hall past him, white shoes squeaking softly on the grey industrial carpet. He followed her long, slim, white-sheathed legs with admiration; he'd always been a sucker for tall women. His wife Peg was five-feet-ten, a half inch taller than Mallor, himself. The nurse turned into room 529 and Mallor, disappointed, went back to staring at a watercolor of flowers and trees hanging on the opposite side of the hall; it was an attempt at impressionism and a complete failure.

"Officer," a voice called. "Will you help me with the report?"

Mallor looked up and saw the nurse motioning to him from outside room 529. He stood up and looked into Julie's room, where Casey was reading under the concentrated yellow glow of a high-intensity light. She smiled wearily back at him, and satisfied, he moved down the hall toward 529. He was tired, his uniform with all its police paraphernalia hung heavily on him, and he debated on calling the stationhouse and getting a midnight replacement. He was no good to anyone in this shape. He also wanted to call Rachel at the house, just to check in.

The nurse wasn't in the doorway so he swung left into the dark room. The bed on the wall to his left was unmade. And, suddenly, a tiny voice inside him said, *"Wrong!"*

At that instant, the metal door of the patient's closet swung open behind him and before he could move or speak or even think, a taut wire bit savagely into his neck and he was jerked helplessly back against an unknown body. His fingers desperately grabbed out at the wire ripping into his flesh, which, in seconds, had already begun to cut into his trachea. Panicking, he thrashed his legs about wildly. He heard his attacker grunt and the incredible force around his neck seemed to increase. His hands gave up the wire and grabbed back at the attacker's hair, but he was too quick and snapped his head away.

Scotty Mallor heard his own gagging sound and dully realized he was going to lose. The wire around his neck seemed white-hot. He was burning up, the pain, something awful and huge. His hands finally grabbed and held the attacker's hair but his strength was going fast now, as the pressure on his neck cut off his air. He heard another grunt, then his own pitifully, frighteningly faint choking. Darkness poured in on him and in his last moment of consciousness he thought, *I love you, Peggy.*

This his windpipe snapped like a brittle twig.

The Cyclone climbed inexorably toward the final peak, chains clicking smoothly, a perfect killing machine. He felt strong, unconquerable, the beast inside him growling in anticipation. A rivulet of saliva spilled out of one corner of his mouth onto the floor, next to the lifeless body.

He closed the door to room 529 and moved with perfect grace and economy to the window. Power, like electricity, surged through his sinews as he pushed it open. He could smell her putrid stench, sense her heat, now finally, so close.

The Cyclone rose into the night air as he went through the window and dropped onto the roof that bordered on the maternity wing of the old hospital.

44

Danbury Hospital,
Danbury, Connecticut

TIME AND AGAIN SHE HAD THE SENSATION OF GOING in and out, the drugs forcing her back beyond the reach of reality, her strong will fighting back until she was again on the brink of waking.

In the dream, her baby was talking to her. It was a man-child and he was afraid. She could feel his fear as tiny fingers scraped at the walls of her womb. Her unborn child thrashed about as if he knew he could get out and save himself before it was too late. They were one spirit, one consciousness and both suffocating from the fear. In the blackness of the dream it was time for him to come, and she heard his voice calling out to her.

And then the voice was different, repeating over and over: *"Wake up Mommy, wake up."*

Suddenly, the dream was gone; her eyes sprang open and she was staring into two mad, dancing eyes hovering inches over her head.

As she started to scream, a hand clamped over her mouth. *"Don't move, Mommy."* Desperately she twisted her head and saw Casey, bound hand and foot, white tape over her mouth, eyes wild in her head.

"Don't do that, Mommy," he said, ripping more white tape off a roll and slapping it over her mouth, then tightly around the back of her head.

"Look at me, Mommy," the voice said. *"See how special I am."*

She stared up at him, and her eyes locked onto his face.

"Don't I look special, Mommy?" he whispered in sing-song.

Mesmerized, Julie saw the curving lines where his mouth drew back into the cheeks, the way the eyes narrowed when he grinned; all at once she saw beyond the sick, Mad-hatter expression to an impish, twinkling countenance she had known before. She'd seen that smile so often, so long ago, now. She'd loved it at first, then eventually had come to distrust it. Even despise it. It was TJ's smile, and somehow in her hysteria she had transplanted it onto the face of the madman who wanted to kill her. He smiled again, his eyes glittering madly down at her. His face came down and she flinched, pressing herself back into the pillow. His breath washed warm over her, and the grin grew wider on his pale face. *"Dr. Kreuger sends his regards,"* he cackled.

The name Dr. Kreuger rang in her mind like a huge bell pounded by a hammer. She shook her head, and the awful grin came again.

"I am your worst nightmare," he whispered, his lips suddenly pressing lasciviously at her ear. *"Your most terrible secret, Mommy."*

269

She twisted away as his hand snaked out and grabbed her around the chin, brutally yanking her back to him.

Her mind raced away from what could not be. And then TJ's smile was there again and the monstrous, impossible truth seized a corner of her consciousness.

The lips were at her ear again, mocking her. *"You tried to kill me, but I wouldn't die."*

All at once, the slim shred of doubt that lingered in her sanity was gone. It wasn't just that it *could* be true, it *was* true. He couldn't look as he did, like TJ, and *know* about Dr. Kreuger. He was who he said he was, an insane killer, a half-man, half-child, who'd found his natural mother and come to kill her because she had tried to kill him. He was her own aborted son from twenty years ago, somehow alive!

It was all so simple and terrifying, and when she finally accepted it, her mind seemed to seize up. Paralyzed and helpless, she looked up at him in revulsion at the idea of it all, in dread of the sick justice to come. And for the most fleeting instant, a sense of deep guilt, mixed with the smallest shred of . . . affection?

"You've been a bad Mommy," he murmured, *"a bad Mommy."*

"Police!!" Pierce bellowed as he sprinted from the admissions desk across the wide lobby of the hospital toward a closing elevator door. A startled, heavyset woman inside looked out at him, hesitated, then let the doors close. Pierce skidded up to the closed doors, and slammed his fist into them with a curse. He whirled toward an alarmed security guard. "I'm a police officer!!" he screamed. "Where are the stairs?"

The guard backed away from him and pointed down a hall, past the elevators.

Pierce raced down the hall, yanked open a door, and went up the stairs, two at a time. Moundsey would have other officers on their way in a matter of minutes—he just didn't know whether they had any minutes left.

Gasping for breath he made the fifth floor, and willed himself to slow down. He pulled open the corridor door noiselessly and stuck his head through. Except for his own breathing the floor was silent. Room 531 was at the other end of the hall. The chair in front of it was unoccupied and Pierce swore under his breath. He ran down the hall, past the nurses' station, staying on his toes to reduce noise. The door of room 531 was closed. Every human instinct compelled him to smash into the door and get to Julie in case *he* was already in there. Every professional instinct told him, *wait! Get control. Think it out.*

The bottom of the door fit so close to the floor that there was no way of telling whether the light was on or not. If *he* was in there, a few seconds' delay might be a few too many. Maybe it was already too late. But if he'd planned it out this far, he wouldn't be surprised by Pierce's entry. He'd be waiting, and then there'd be no one to save Julie.

Pierce snuck to the door and placed an ear to it. Through the fiberboard veneer he could hear the vaguest of exchanges. The voices sounded high-pitched, like two women talking. *Thank God!* he thought. Julie and Casey. Then, just before he took his head away, he thought he heard one of the voices call out. *In pain or fear?* Ever so gently, he placed his hand on the door knob. It would not turn. And that was when he realized that the door to room 531 was closed when it should have been open. Unless a doctor was with her, he'd left a clear order to keep her door open at all times.

Pierce dashed to the nurses' station.

"Is there a doctor with Julie Weston?" he barked.

The night nurse shook her head. "No rounds, tonight."

"When did you last see the police guard?"

She looked down at Mallor's empty chair, understanding and alarm occurring in her, simultaneously. "Fifteen minutes, maybe twenty."

"I need to get into Room 531. Is there any other way besides the door?" Pierce asked, knowing now that something *had* to be wrong. Mallor would never leave his spot for fifteen minutes. Never. "What about the windows?" he demanded, his mind racing.

She answered immediately, pointing to the nearest room. "There."

Moments later Pierce landed on the roof. He ran past the double windows of each room, counting as he went, until he reached 530. *Did the killer know he would be doing this, too?* Then he dropped to his knees and crawled toward 531. As he moved forward, he felt like a fool, the wooden doll at the end of the marionette's string. Finally, the counting led him to the window of the right room, and the window was in its down position. Locked? Was it even the kind that *could* open?

Underneath the window, he drew his gun and waited, gathering himself as he strained to hear sounds from the room. At first there was nothing, but as he started to rise, he heard it. A child's voice, saying— no—singing, *"Bad Mommy, bad Mommy."* He felt the breath rush out of his lungs and he gulped for air. Then, slowly, he raised his eyes to window-level.

His first look registered a normal scene. Bed, water pitcher, intravenous bottles. There was a tall blonde nurse leaning over a patient, and he found himself wondering why the desk nurse hadn't mentioned that the nurse was in with Julie when he had asked about a doctor. Then he saw the tape over Casey's mouth, the lamp wire around her hands as she sat rigid in her chair.

His eyes darted to the nurse again and traveled the lines of her face. He forced his vision to focus on the short, straight nose, the brows like two golden lines of wheat, too thick for the delicate feminine cheekbones. He looked at her cheeks, themselves, then lower to the throat. There was a slight texture where it should have been completely smooth. It was a hardly-visible section of blond beard that had been missed in shaving just under the chin.

Pierce shuddered and dropped back below the window. He readied himself. He was only going to have one shot at it. It was going to look like a woman, but it wasn't. It wasn't even a man anymore, just some fiendish animal. In his entire seventeen-year police career, he had never killed anyone, had never really known if he could, should the time come. Now, such thoughts were extraneous. His only focus was on his chances for success. Gun gripped firmly, but not too tightly, not too tensely, he lifted himself, prepared to fire.

"*Bad Mommy,*" the child's voice in a nurse's uniform scolded again. "*Bad Mommy must die.*"

An obscene, huge hunting knife appeared in his hand and Julie knew the nightmare wasn't a nightmare at all. Her mind spun out of control to Robert, then Casey, and finally to the baby. All she loved in this world—all about to end. Maybe it was better this way, better than being left alone. She prayed it wouldn't hurt too much.

But the will to go on rose in her, past any other thought, past any other connection to family, to the ache of emptiness, even to her unborn baby. Frantically, she rehearsed the one feeble, last defense she'd been able to muster in the panic since his entrance from the unguarded hallway. Unconsciously, she flexed the fingers of her right hand to shed some of the tingling sensation caused by the intravenous tubes.

There was nothing left to do, nothing else to hope for. She tensed her body in preparation, her eyes clinging to the knife hovering above her swollen naval and the mad face behind it, staring at her belly in nightmarish fascination. Then, slowly, another face rose up like an apparition behind the killer's.

Her eyes instinctively widened in surprise, and as

the killer spun around, she knew she'd made a mistake.

The thick window shattered under the force of the gun's handle, but in the time it had taken Pierce to break the glass, the white-clad figure was off the bed and hurling himself toward him. Pierce grabbed the gun with his other hand to right it, but even then he saw the pointed end of the nurse's shoe coming at his face. If he ducked it would give the killer enough time to reach Julie—there wasn't enough time to aim and shoot.

The gun exploded just before the foot struck him at the bridge of his nose, and he heard the killer cry out as he, himself, went reeling down among the pipes and tar of the hospital roof, a fiery pain engulfing his entire body.

Julie tried to scream but made no sound as the killer, who looked like TJ, who looked like Julie, turned slowly from the window. There was blood oozing from the part of his forehead that had been shredded by Pierce's bullet. Someone was pounding at the door. The killer wiped at the blood with a sleeve, only to smear it further. There was blood dripping on the floor, then the bed, then on her.

He came over her, smiling in triumph, his eyes bright, dancing. He leaned over her, the knife now in striking position just over her belly.

"I was in there!!" he suddenly screamed out, weaving above her breasts.

The bloody hand went backwards for a second, over his shoulders, higher, starting to rise over his head.

Julie took the last few seconds of life and spent them looking to her right. There, at just about the level of his head, was the gleaming object she had reserved for this moment. Quickly she raised her right arm off the bed and felt the cold bottom of the rounded glass container. Instantly she closed her hand over it and tightened her grip. She saw the killer's hand stop in mid-air just before its last descent downward, but by then her own hand had started forward, holding the hard, intravenous bottle. She thought about Robert, clinging to life; about Casey, vulnerable in the chair; about the life inside her; Pierce, all of it, and her strength rose with each indignity until she knew she could do it, announcing it with a whining, animal howling of rage. She threw the bottle forward. It crashed into the side of his skull.

Taken off-guard, he reeled and fell back with a surprised shriek of pain, losing his balance and falling against the wall near the open window. The knife landed a second later nearer the door that now was being splintered from the outside. Desperately, Julie twisted toward the bedside table and grabbed a second saline bottle. Already his feet were under him as she struggled to her knees on the bed over him. Using both hands, she hurled the bottle down at his head, but he shifted at the last instant and the bottle smashed against his shoulder, harmlessly.

Shaking his head to clear it, he was up, his bared teeth bright against the bloody mass that now covered his whole face. His inhuman eyes locked on hers and for the barest of moments everything stopped. Then he threw himself at her, slamming her head back as he thrust his strong, thick fingers around her neck.

She felt his weight on her, the thumbs pressing into the softness of her neck. Julie thrashed feebly, her strength and will finally expended, and felt the life leaving her.

A tremendous explosion rocked the room and Julie felt the weight suddenly lift off her, saw the fiendish mask go slack, the eyes close forever. Sobbing and gasping, she saw Mel Pierce, an arm wrapped around the stanchion between the two windows, a smoking gun in his hand. He stopped moving long enough to let a small smile struggle to his lips. Then he groaned and fell back onto the roof.

Epilogue

THE WARM AIR WAS MORE LIKE SUMMER THAN LATE fall, but it carried a rich scent of dry leaves. Above the gleaming white clapboard house, giant sugar maples had already turned shades of yellow and reddish-brown. Detective Mel Pierce stopped once more, before slowly descending the last steep section of lawn. He turned and looked back. It had been his first trip to Connecticut since the child's birth. His eyes lingered a while on the four of them. They were sitting close to each other, clustered around a small garden of freshly-dug earth in which the new mother had somehow found the time to plant bulbs for spring. The father was holding the baby now, but soon it would be someone else's turn. Pierce made a small sound and thought about his empty bachelor's apartment in New York. Then he turned and, winded, got into his car. He was not, he told himself, quite ready yet to defend his Mid-North division handball championship.

Pierce inhaled the country air deeply and started the car. He waved back at them.

"Drive carefully," he heard Julie call, "you're a godfather now. You've got responsibilities."

Pierce grinned and flashed a thumbs-up sign. As he drove off he felt as if he was saying good-bye to his family.

278

Robert handed his sleeping baby to Julie with the exaggerated care of someone unaccustomed to infants. He had been home for only two weeks, but he could finally feel his strength returning. His recovery, the doctors had said, was miraculous. He'd told them that he was "highly motivated."

Casey noticed his clumsiness with the baby and giggled affectionately, then turned to her mother, who'd brought the baby close to her lips. Julie could feel the warmth coming through the small bundle as she examined the miniature face. As she watched in delight, the sun came from behind a cloud and bathed his soft skin in shades of amber and rose. For a moment, the brightness made him stir, and when she pressed her lips to his cheek his eyes opened and he struggled to focus. She drifted into his eyes, too, and they communed in silence until he broke into a cock-eyed smile and she threw back her head in laughter.

For the first time in many weeks there was no thought in her mind about what had happened since the baby had begun to form within her. In fact, there was nothing to trouble the unusually warm October afternoon. There was only softness and joy. There was only Robert and Casey and her baby, and the house, the trees, and the grass. And the unquestionable fact that Robert Weston Montgomery, Jr. was going to look exactly like her.

Innocent People Caught In The Grip Of TERROR!